AMERICAN Diaries

Willow Chase

KANSAS TERRITORY, 1847

—∞∞∞—

by Kathleen Duey

D0107666

—∞∞∞—

Aladdin Paperbacks

For Richard
For Ever

25 Years of Magical Reading

ALADDIN PAPERBACKS
EST. 1972

First Aladdin Paperbacks edition, February 1997
Copyright © 1997 by Kathleen Duey

Aladdin Paperbacks
An imprint of Simon & Schuster
Children's Publishing Division
1230 Avenue of the Americas
New York, NY 10020

Library of Congress Cataloging-in-Publication Data
Duey, Kathleen.
Willow Chase, Kansas Territory, 1847 / Kathleen Duey. —1st
Aladdin Paperbacks ed.
p.   cm. — (American diaries ; #5)
Summary: In 1847, when her mother's remarriage sends them on a difficult journey to California, Willow is swept overboard fording the South Platte River and must survive and search for her family.
ISBN 0-689-81355-4 (pbk.)
[1. Overland journeys to the Pacific—Fiction. 2. Frontier and pioneer life—West (U.S.)—Fiction. 3. Survival—Fiction. 4. Remarriage—Fiction.] I. Title. II. Series.
PZ7.D8694Wi   1997
[Fic]—dc20   96-35021
CIP   AC

June 3, 1847,
South Platte River, Kansas Territory

These last three storms have swelled the South Platte River so high that the men are now afraid to cross. They are also afraid to wait. We are far behind schedule now and will be caught in the onset of cold weather if we do not hurry. Even worse, there is no grass here, and the poor oxen are near starving, as well as the mules and horses. Four beef cattle died this morning. Mr. Hansen says we will follow downstream tomorrow in hope of grass and a fording place.

I spent nearly an hour this evening, while tending the cookfire, pulling burrs from Fancy's coat and paws. Foolish thing, he ran down along the riverbank before I could stop him and is very sorry now he didn't heed my calls. The burrs have the oddest scent—like pine trees and camphor—and his coat stills smells of them.

Anna is mending, I think. No fever yet, thank God. Oh, what I would give to have been able to reach out, to stop her jumping from the wagon—so that the wheel had not gone over her poor foot. I can hardly bear to look at it when Mama changes the wrappings and I must hold Anna's hands to help her keep from moving. Anna is only ten years old, but braver than I could be. Her pain must be terrible, but she doesn't complain.

Levin and Jordan are both doing what they can to help with Anna's chores so that they do not all fall on me, even though they both have plenty of their own work. I am grateful.

Mama spoke with me yesterday about Mr. Hansen. I am trying but still cannot think of him as our stepfather. I wish Mama had not married him. He is so strict, so stern that, try as I may, I find great difficulty in liking him at all. He hates Fancy.

Passed eleven graves today. One of them was tiny, a baby, I am sure. Five of them had been disturbed. Wolves or Indians—we did not stop to look. A month ago we would have, but now everyone dreads even small delays. We must find grass—the cattle are weakening. God willing we will all get to California. I hope that by the time I write again we shall be across this wide river, all safe, and on our way. More than being afraid of the sickness and Indians, worse than anything, I hate the rivers. Oh, how I dread this swift, muddy water.

CHAPTER ONE

It was close to dawn but still dark. Willow lay motionless. She could feel her diary beneath her pillow and she reached under to touch the smooth, cool canvas cover. She was supposed to be keeping a journal of the westward journey—that's why Auntie Rose had bought the diary for her. But it was turning out to be more than that. Usually she just folded it into her blankets. But she was beginning to think she should hide it; her mother would be very upset if she read it now.

Willow wanted to turn over, but she didn't. Fancy was asleep at the foot of her bed, curled up on her legs. Any movement would awaken him, and he would start to whimper and whine to be let down out of the wagon. That would start the day off with everyone in a bad humor, especially Mr. Hansen. He hated to have anything upset his routines—which meant that on this trip, he had been stern and discomfited most of the time. How could anyone plan for hail the size of hen's eggs or windstorms that rattled the wagons and tore the canvas covers like invisible claws?

Willow stared toward the wide platform that served her mother and Mr. Hansen as a bed. It ran the width of the wagon, just behind the driver's seat. Beneath it, sacks of flour and meal were stacked next to neatly folded tents, India rubber ground cloths, and the equally rubbery gutta-percha covers used for keeping water off the flour when it rained.

Outside, cattle were beginning to shift within the great circle of wagons that served as their nightly corral. That meant dawn was close. Willow was glad. She hated sleeping inside the wagon. She yawned, staring up at the canvas that covered the curved bows that topped the wagon. Inside like this, the wagon always felt so crowded, so close.

Except for their beds, there was not a single inch that was not stacked with *something* needed for the journey. Willow could imagine every item and the exact place where it was packed. After all, she had helped load and unload this wagon at least a dozen times since they had left Missouri. And every morning they had to repack what they had taken out the night before to clear the beds off for sleeping.

"Willow?"

It was Anna's tiny whisper, barely audible, so as not to waken Willow if she hadn't already wakened on her own.

"I'm not asleep," Willow breathed, and she heard Anna sigh. No doubt her pain had put an end to her rest. Willow felt a pang of anguish. Her younger sister was the sweetest-natured person she had ever known. It seemed wrong that so gentle a spirit should have to suffer so.

"Anna? You all right?" Levin whispered from the boys' bed.

Willow smiled a little in the dark. Levin was the eldest, and he was becoming more and more like their father had been—kind and good. "Is it morning?" Levin's question was answered by a muted cock's crow from across the camp.

Anna made a little sound of pain, and Willow longed to reach out and take her hand. Normally, they would have shared the bed that Willow was in.

Since Anna's accident, they had slept separately; their mother was afraid Willow would bump Anna's poor, crushed foot in the night. Anna had her own little cot now, crammed in on the side of the wagon that held the India rubber sugar sacks and the dried vegetables Mr. Hansen had mail ordered from a company in Paris, France. Her mother and Mr. Hansen had argued about the expense of the dried vegetables, but he had won, of course.

She should think of him as her stepfather, not Mr. Hansen, Willow reminded herself. She had promised her mother she would try harder. And whether she liked it or not, that's what Mr. Hansen was. Her stepfather.

Willow blinked hard against the tears that pressed into her eyes. Her mother had married Mr. Hansen nearly six months before—and Willow still could not find a way to like him, much less to respect and love him the way she had loved her own father.

"Willow? Shall we get up?" Levin's whisper was a little louder this time.

"I suppose." Willow looked up at the canvas. It was getting lighter out—she could just see the ribs of the wagon roof. The rooster crowed again. But for almost a full minute longer, she didn't move. She lay very still, soaking up the warmth and comfort of her hard little bed. Once she moved, the work would begin, and it wouldn't end until it was dark again.

Jordan would sleep until noon, through a hailstorm, until he was an old man, if he were allowed. So would Anna, if her foot were not so painful. Willow and Levin were always the first to wake up. It had been that way at home, too; it hadn't just been true for the journey.

"Willow?" Levin stirred on the bed he shared with Jordan. "We ought to get up."

"I suppose," Willow said slowly. She moved very slightly and felt the warm circle that was Fancy lighten and shrink as he raised his head. She couldn't really see him yet, but his quick movement told her he was awake. And once Fancy was awake, she had no choice.

Willow slid out of her bed and shivered as the cool morning air touched her skin. She reached for Fancy, petting him and raising him to brush his warm, furry cheek against her own. Then she set him down. He whimpered quietly and she flinched, hurrying to pull her red calico dress on over her chemise. Her shoes were outside the wagon with everyone elses'.

Carrying Fancy under one arm, Willow walked sideward, making her way to the back of the wagon.

The canvas wagon cover was gathered in a puckered ring by a cord that was tied to a peg set into the side board. She bent to reach for the end. Just then, a cow lowed close to the wagon, and Fancy let out one quick, startled yap.

"What in tarnation. . . ?"

Willow drew in a quick breath and fumbled with the string, wishing she had a spare hand to clasp around Fancy's muzzle. He barked again, and Willow heard the sharp, critical throat clearing from the front of the wagon. Mr. Hansen, her *step-father*, was awake and letting her know that he didn't appreciate it.

Willow managed to loosen the tie cord, then leaned out and put Fancy through the hole, bracing herself against the wagon gate. She half crouched, lowering him to within a foot of the ground before she let go. He hit with a happy yelp and raced off.

"If that dog ever causes a stampede, running through the stock like that, there'll be hell to pay."

Willow straightened. "Yes, sir. But the cattle are used to him."

Mr. Hansen cleared his throat again, a rough, irritating sound. "Cattle will stampede for no reason at all, Willow. Someday he will startle them and there's no telling what will come of it."

Willow clenched her jaw and stepped over the wagon gate.

"Get the fire built up, Willow," her mother called from inside the wagon. "Breakfast early, then we can be off."

Willow kicked at the ground on her way to the fire pit they had used the night before. Off to where? Another ten miles downstream? Sometimes, she felt as if the journey would never end, that the endless, empty miles would surround them forever. Willow poked at the ashes with a stick. Red glowed from beneath. She walked back to the wagon and pulled a few small pieces of deadwood from the hayrick Mr. Hansen had rigged up on the sideboard. That was one of the chores the boys had taken over for Anna. Now they both looked for firewood as constantly as Willow did, throwing it into the hayrick as the wagon moved over the road. They had been burning wet wood for three days, and the fires had been sooty and smoky.

Willow stirred the coals free of soft, white, smothering ash and laid her wood on them, slimmest pieces first. Then, while the heat of the coals dried the kindling, she went to the back of the wagon and reached into the moss sack. Moss was her mother's favorite tinder. At every slow-moving creek they had to gather moss and then hang banners of it in the wagon to dry. That meant packing and unpacking it every morning until it was completely dry and could be stuffed into an old flour sack. Willow hated handling the slippery moss when it was wet and smelled of fish and snails. But she had to admit it made wonderful tinder.

She took two handfuls of the dried moss and tucked it between the kindling and the coals and blew on it gently. It started to smoke almost immediately. Willow stared at the glowing coals and kept blowing gently, steadily, her breaths timed perfectly from long practice so that she wouldn't get dizzy. She didn't like using the hand bellows unless she had to. It was just one more thing to unpack.

Willow sat up straight and watched the tiny spirals of smoke tickle at the wood. Once they got to California they would find land and settle. Then things would be better. Anna's foot would heal. It would. And Levin and Jordan could get ponies and ride out together to hunt in the woods above their hay fields. Their farm would be beautiful, with fine cattle and neighbors and a town with a school and a church and stores. And friends.

A small flame sprang up, and Willow nursed it along with her breath until it was snapping at the kindling, spreading down the underside of the wood.

"Boil water first for coffee, then start a second pot for the corn mush."

Willow straightened so quickly that she felt dizzy for a second. "I didn't know you were there."

Mr. Hansen smiled tightly. "I was whistling. You must have been lost in a daydream. Where's your dog?"

Willow glanced around. She didn't want to admit that she had lost track of Fancy. No one else was supposed to have to worry about him even for a minute. That was the promise she had made to her mother in exchange for permission to bring him at all.

She made a vague gesture. "He's close by somewhere. . . ."

"Willow?" Willow turned to see her mother leaning from the back of the wagon, her shawl wrapped over her nightgown. "Would you fetch a cup of water for Anna?"

Willow nodded, excusing herself from Mr. Hansen. She took the empty cup from her mother and walked around to the far side of the wagon to the open water barrel. She pulled the cork and filled the cup without spilling a single drop. They had gone four days without any water once. She could still remember the awful, swollen mass of her tongue, the incredible craving for a drink. She replaced the cork and caught the last drops in the cup.

"Morning. That for Anna?"

Willow looked up. Jordan was coming out the front of the wagon, crawling over the buckboard seat. Levin followed. Both their shirts were soiled. Laundry day would have to be soon. Willow dreaded the thought of pounding heavy, wet clothes on river rocks. It was getting harder for her mother to bend over, and now Anna wouldn't be able to help at all.

"Come on, Levin," Jordan said, pulling at his brother's arm. "Let's see if we can be the first hitched up this morning."

Willow shook her head at them. "Why hurry? The men will have to have their 'do we go farther south' argument. Let the oxen graze until halfway through breakfast anyway."

Levin nodded. "She's right." He turned at the sound of a commotion across the camp.

Willow hurried to the back of the wagon, handing the full cup of water to her mother. Then she whirled and set off at a run, lifting her skirt with both hands. She ran along the edge of the circle, swerving to avoid other families, other cookfires. Somewhere in all the shouts she was pretty sure she had heard a high-pitched yapping.

CHAPTER TWO

Willow skidded to a stop near the Banners' wagon on the far side of the big circle. There were twenty-three wagons in the train, and the Banner family was one she liked. They had a wagonload of small children who had Fancy surrounded this morning. They were just petting him, it looked like, but there were so many hands and so many dirty little faces that it had scared Fancy, and now he was barking to make them back off a little.

Mrs. Banner was standing with a skillet raised high in one hand. She was beating at it with a ladle held in the other. "Come now for your breakfast, or

I will have to throw it out." Her voice was hoarse, her face cheerful and stolid. Willow often saw her pulling her various children around by one arm or the front of a jacket, cajoling them into doing this small chore or that.

"I'd better take my dog now," Willow called out over the racket. Mrs. Banner smiled at her and nodded, then raised the skillet and rang it like a gong again.

"Last chance! Those who are hungry ought to come right now."

The giggling circle of children began to dissolve. Willow whistled, the special high-pitched whistle that she used only for Fancy. His ears perked up, and he faced her. Then he leapt in a circle on his back legs, showing off. Willow had to smile. Fancy's tricks had been the only thing that could make her laugh in the first few months after her father had died. Fancy kept it up until the Banner children giggled again and ran off to breakfast.

"Come on, Fancy," Willow called, and the little dog ran straight toward her, leaping so high and so perfectly into her arms that she caught him without bending over at all. It was a trick they had worked on for hours when he was a pup. Willow glanced up to see Mrs. Banner looking at her from her perennial post next to the cookfire. She smiled wistfully and went back to ladling. Several of her children had seen Fancy's leap, and they drifted back toward Willow, the oldest boy carrying a tin plate of steaming flapjacks. "Your mama said last chance," Willow reminded them. They scattered, chasing one another back to the cookfire.

Willow glanced at the next wagon. The preacher's wife, Mrs. Holliday, was standing with her hands on her hips. Willow couldn't tell if she was glaring at the Banner children or at her, and she didn't wait to find out. Mrs. Holliday was angry that her husband had led her into the wasteland territories bordering the United States of America. She never got tired of telling people how much she missed Ohio and her parents and her sisters and everything else that her husband had made her leave behind.

Holding Fancy tightly to keep him still, Willow walked back toward her own wagon. Mr. Hansen was bent over the hitch, working on the whiffletree. He straightened. "What was that about?"

"The Banner children were trying to play with him but there are so many of them that—"

"And what in the world was he doing clear over there?"

Willow looked right into his eyes. She knew that he preferred her to look aside when he was scolding her for something, but lately she couldn't make herself do it.

"I want that dog of yours kept close, Willow. It isn't that I am cruel or that I don't understand how fond you are of him."

Willow nodded. She had heard this lecture at least thirty times. She could recite it almost by heart. Next he would talk about Fancy damaging someone's property.

"What if he had made the cattle stampede and someone's wagon had been damaged? That would be our fault. People might expect us to pay for the repairs."

Willow nodded again, still looking directly into his eyes.

"What if, God forgive me for saying it, someone was hurt because of him? Then what? Are we to expect these people to travel with us if we keep an animal that presents a danger to everyone here?"

Willow shook her head. "But he doesn't."

"He does if you can't keep hold of him," Mr. Hansen said very quietly. "Willow, your mother has enough to worry her just now."

Willow finally dropped her gaze. He was right about that much. She glanced toward the cookfire, where her mother stood, bent heavily forward over the fire. Mr. Hansen gripped her shoulder for an instant, then released her when she looked back at him. "Keep a close watch on Fancy. At the least, all this dog chasing has made you forget how awkward chores have become for your mother. Best get on over to help."

Willow nodded again, feeling guilty. Her mother was pregnant, and stooping to cook over the fire was hard for her. Willow walked away from Mr. Hansen, trying to imagine what it was going to be like to have a new brother or sister—one who was only a *half* brother or sister. She set Fancy down, pushing her hair back as she stood straight. Wet weather made it so tangled—sometimes it was almost impossible to comb.

"Let me do that," Willow said, and accepted her mother's grateful smile as she took the ladle from her. She knelt on the painted canvas ground cloth her mother had spread near the fire and served Levin a plate of boiled corn mush, then Jordan. They argued over the molasses tin for a minute, then got things worked out quickly as Mr. Hansen walked past with the first yoke of oxen.

"I can use a hand when you boys have eaten."

Willow spooned mush for herself and poured as much molasses as she dared upon it, then set the tin back in the box that held their kitchen. It fit perfectly between the cast-iron frying pan and the salt can. The box was neat and orderly now. Both she and her mother preferred it that way. They rarely mislaid or had to look for anything for more than a moment. Anna was messier. Willow usually had to reorder the box after Anna helped. But Anna hadn't been able to help since she had gotten hurt.

Willow turned over her cracker crate to sit upon. Fancy curled up at her feet, looking upward hopefully. She always saved some little treat for him to lick from her fingers when she was finished. He liked molasses, which Willow teased him about. He also liked baked apples with cinnamon, and custard and cream, and popovers, and dainties, and all manner of fancy foods, which was how he had gotten his name.

Willow looked at the lump of mush in her tin. There was a little sand in it, but that was usual. They often cooked in windy weather or had to scoop everything up and run to escape rain or hail. It was impossible to keep the food as clean as one would in a kitchen at home. Maybe the next bag of cornmeal would stay clean, if they were lucky and had only fine weather.

The mush was hot and Willow had to stir it briskly before she could put even one bite in her mouth. Levin and Jordan turned over their crates and sat down to eat. They all ate fast and in silence.

"Willow," her mother said.

She looked up from her plate to see her mother extending a slab of bacon, dripping with savory grease. Willow held out her tin, and her mother plopped the meat on top of her mush. Willow pierced it with her fork and lifted it to cool the bacon with her breath. The boys took their bacon and wolfed it down. Willow watched Levin chewing for a few seconds, his cheeks puffed out like a squirrel's. She had decided long ago that his lips and tongue must be made of iron. He drank hot coffee straight down, too. More than any of the rest of the family, Levin seemed comfortable on the journey, as though he belonged in this lonely country with its endless skies.

Willow stirred her mush, still watching her brother. Mrs. Banner had told her a story about a family who had gone from Indiana to Oregon by wagon. Once they got there, their youngest daughter refused to sleep inside the cabin they built. She was terrified of being closed in, of the sound of the grandfather clock they had carried all across the weary miles, of the cookstove, of everything that made up a normal life. At three, a third of her life had been spent camping from a wagon, and it was all she remembered.

Willow glanced at her mother, who no longer cautioned any of them to stay clean or to eat politely. She was still relatively clean and groomed, for the wagon train, but Willow knew she would be laughed at by all of their old friends if they could see her now. Her hair was wispy, trailing down her neck and cheeks, her hands as brown as a farmer's from the sun. Her bonnet and apron were faded and stained with prairie clay.

They had been passed by one set of travelers just outside St. Louis who had brought hired cooks and herders and a personal maidservant with them on the trek. Those women had still looked fresh and proper, as though the journey were one long picnic.

Willow took another bite of her bacon and ate it sideways off the fork. She would be willing to bet those dainty, proud women had since lived through at least one or two adventures that reduced them to looking like most women did on the wagon trails: dirty, tired, and a little scared.

Willow glanced at the sky. The sun was rising clear and fresh in the east, but to the west the clouds lay in a mass along the horizon. It would be pleasant to have a day without rain. But more than that, a dry day would mean that the river would start to lower.

Crossing rivers was awful for Willow. When the water was high, it took every particle of courage she had not to scream and fight when it was her turn to cross. All she could ever see when she looked at roiling brown water was her father, swept downstream, farther and farther. Away forever.

CHAPTER THREE

"Willow? Willow!"

She looked up. Her mother was staring at her. "Take a plate in to Anna, will you?"

Willow nodded and blushed. How could she forget Anna, lying in the wagon waiting for breakfast? She should have taken her a plate first. She stood, tossing Fancy a piece of bacon with molasses on it, quickly downing her last two or three bites of mush. She rubbed her tin plate out with sand three times, until all the stickiness was gone, then held it out for her mother to refill.

Anna was sitting up when Willow came

through the back gate of the wagon. "Oh, wonderful, Willow. I think I can eat a little this morning. You know what I am afraid of?"

Willow smiled as she handed Anna her tin and fork. In pain and cooped up, Anna was better natured than most people when they had no cares at all.

Willow sat carefully on the edge of Anna's cot. "What?"

"Getting the dysentery. *Now*, I mean. I couldn't run when I had to go. I can't even walk. Someone would have to help me use a bucket a dozen times a day. . . ."

They both began to giggle, and Willow put her arm around her sister. "And that helper would be me, of course."

Anna nodded, stirring at her mush. "Of course. Who else would get the honor?"

Willow made a face, imagining it. Anna was using a bucket now, and that was pretty bad. Normal dailies were problem enough. There were no privies, of course. Not out here where the miles went on and on, and the naked, empty country rolled on forever. There weren't even bushes most of the time. There was no privacy, no easy way to bathe or wash up when they were sick.

"Remember Beaver Creek?" Anna asked wistfully.

Willow sighed. "I do." Twice, at slow-running rivers, the women in the train had formed a curved, living curtain of spread skirts, their backs to the river, taking turns until everyone had gotten a chance to have a real bath, with soap and enough time to wash her hair and rinse it thoroughly, luxuriously in the clean, cool water.

Anna dipped her fork in her mush and took a little on the tip of her tongue. Since her accident she had not eaten well at all, and Willow knew their mother was concerned about it. Anna moved her foot slightly, and her face creased with pain. "It really does ache all the time. Mr. Hansen says it will abate soon, but it has not. This is the tenth day."

Willow nodded and tightened her arm around her sister's shoulders. "You are braver about it than I could be."

A sharp yelp from the back of the wagon made Anna smile a little. "Your shadow. Best get him inside so he doesn't stampede Mr. Hansen."

Willow shook her head. "Mother would scold you sure for talk like that."

Anna shrugged and toyed with her food. Willow pushed aside the canvas and knelt, leaning out far enough so that Fancy could leap into her arms. She straightened, hauling him inside.

Willow sat on the edge of Anna's bed and

Fancy curled up near her feet. The bed was really three planks lashed together with two India rubber ground cloths and three or four doubled blankets covering them. Mr. Hansen had placed it near one of the stacks of flour sacks, so Anna could use them as a backrest during the day's ride.

"I would hate riding back here," Willow said, then smiled apologetically. "I meant it when I said that you were much braver than I."

Anna shook her head. "I can hardly refuse, can I? Does it look like rain today?"

"Maybe not, Anna. Not now, at least. There are clouds far off to the west."

"It's worst back here when it rains. They tighten down the cover so it's dark and damp and it smells like mildew."

Willow made a sympathetic sound. The only time she had had to ride in the wagon had come early in the journey when she'd had a fever. Her mother had ridden beside her with a cloth soaked in chamomile water to cool her so the heat in her body wouldn't damage her brain. Fancy whined and stood up. "He smells your breakfast."

Anna wrinkled her nose and leaned a little toward Fancy, peering down at him. "Does Mr. Fancy think that he has me as charmed as he has you?"

Fancy whined again, breaking into a sharp yap at the end. He knew when he was being teased.

"Does he expect a tidbit from *me* as he would from you?" Anna leaned back, feigning sheer disbelief. "How could he think that? Am I ever the one to carry him? Do I let him sleep on top of my legs?"

"Only if it is very cold and he can keep your feet warm for you," Willow said somberly.

Fancy barked at them both, rising to stand on his hind legs.

Anna took a little mush and held it out to him. "I already ate all the bacon, Fancy. I'm sorry."

"He had a little of mine," Willow told her, as Fancy stood with his front paws on the edge of Anna's bed, trying to get up to reach the mush. Willow lifted him and he licked Anna's fingers. Then, somehow, in turning, he skittered to one side in his excitement and stepped on her bandaged foot.

Anna bit back a cry and jackknifed, jerking forward.

Willow swooped Fancy off the bed. "Oh, Anna. I am so sorry." She looked into her sister's face. Anna had gone white. Her lips were pressed together hard, tears brimming in her eyes. A long, agonizing minute passed with Anna holding Willow's hands so tightly that it hurt. Then she slowly let the pressure ease and leaned back, breathing hard.

"It's—a little better now. Getting better, anyway. Oh, Willow, will my foot ever heal? Will I ever be able to walk again?"

Willow held her hands again. "Of course you will. Of course."

"I am just so scared." Anna's eyes were closed. "I mean even before I got hurt, not just about my foot."

Willow nodded. "I am, too. Everything is so . . ." she stopped, searching her mind for a word that would describe the uneasiness that filled her heart every day when she woke and realized that she was a thousand miles from her home and traveling farther yet. This journey had killed her father. Now Anna was hurt, and this was supposed to be the easiest part of the trek. Would it kill them all? They passed graves every day.

Anna wiped at her eyes, dragging in a deep breath. "If the men are right, California will be a wonderful place to live," she said, trying to smile.

Fancy made a piteous sound from the wagon bed. Willow bent to pat him. "Anna knows you didn't mean it. It was my fault, not yours." She pulled him up into her lap but held him close. His familiar warmth was a comfort to her—it had been since the day she had first gotten him.

"Do we cross today?" Anna asked.

"I hope not," Willow said truthfully. "If it were up to me we would make a farm right here, at this camp, and never cross another river. Ever."

Anna smiled. "Father would not want you to speak that way."

Willow nodded, knowing it was true. He would want her to be brave and happy and well. He had loved her very much. And he had wanted to take them all to California.

Willow blinked to ease the stinging in her eyes. They had camped for almost a month in the gentle Indiana hills after he had drowned. They would have gone home eventually, Willow knew. Her mother would not likely have made this trip alone. But then she had met Mr. Hansen.

CHAPTER FOUR

Willow got her bonnet from the wagon and put it on before her mother had to remind her. Breaking down a camp was always harder, somehow, than setting it up. While her mother helped Mr. Hansen adjust the wagon cover, Willow walked back and forth to the wagon, replacing the boxes of spare wheel spokes and rims, the three shovels, the remaining baskets of apples, and the rest of the household goods she had unpacked the night before.

Anna smiled at Willow every time she appeared with an armload, but Willow could see that her smile was strained. Fancy followed her back and forth, cheerful even after he realized that she was going no farther than the wagon gate. She did not lift him up into the wagon again. She prayed silently that Fancy had not made Anna's foot worse. After eight or ten trips, everything but the kitchen was reloaded, settled into place tightly so that the all-day jolting of the wagon wouldn't cause anything to slide dangerously—especially now that Anna had to ride inside. Only then did Willow look around to see how the other families were doing.

The Campbells, who had been next to them all night, were nearly packed, but they had two grown sons and two daughters, with the younger a big, strong girl of fourteen. And Mrs. Campbell was a wonder. She seemed to have enough energy and gumption for three women. She almost never got sick, and if she had to rest from heavier work, she'd pull out some mending to keep her hands busy.

Besides the Campbells', most of the wagons still had at least a few boxes and bags stacked beside their campfires. Relieved that she wasn't behind, Willow returned to her work. As Mr. Hansen backed the wheeler oxen into place, Willow poured the grease from the frying pan over the remaining mush, then set it aside while she sand-scoured the frying pan. Once it was clean, she set the heavy iron pan into the kitchen box. She had saved the boiling pot for last, so that the mush left in it would be completely cool. Willow caught her mother's eye and smiled in gratitude. Every morning, her mother made sure there was something left for Fancy's breakfast.

"Come on, come on, then. Hurry now." Mr. Hansen's already rough voice was impatient. Willow looked up. He was already almost finished harnessing the second yoke of oxen—and he hadn't been talking to her. It looked as though Levin was slow at fastening his side of the harness buckles. As Willow watched, he grew clumsier and slower under Mr. Hansen's critical eye. At last, Levin jammed the rump strap through its buckle and pulled the catch tight.

Willow was happy to see the oxen. Mr. Hansen had used the mule team while it was raining—they were better at pulling the wagon when the roads turned to rainwater slop and quicksand pudding. The fact that he was hitching up the oxen meant he was expecting no more rain, guessing that the road would firm up as they went southwest.

Just then Brownie, the near-side-wheel ox, lowered her huge head and grunted, shaking her thick neck as much as the wooden yoke would allow. She was getting harder and harder to catch and resisted harnessing. Mr. Hansen reached out and slapped her shoulder, hard. She did not flinch or stop her head shaking. Mr. Hansen swore softly but did not strike Brownie again.

That was one good thing about him, Willow admitted to herself as Fancy ate his mush and bacon grease from the pot. Some of the men whipped their teams mercilessly. Even where the trail was so steep that the wagons had to be emptied and raised with ropes, Mr. Hansen only snapped the whip or lashed it lightly along the oxen's backs to startle them forward. He would shout at them often and shake the reins, but he almost never whipped them.

"Get a little grain for Brownie," Mr. Hansen directed Levin, turning to go catch up the last two oxen. "See if you can calm her down."

Willow used the spoon to loosen the last bit of mush for Fancy. Mr. Hansen was careful to use good saddlecloths and was always checking the mules for sores and bruises. Not one of their animals had died so far. Mr. Hansen had read several books about the westward journey and had learned something new from each one.

Willow cleaned the boiling pot, then gathered the stray utensils and the pot rags. Fancy went to lie down beside the wagon. He knew better than to lie close to the wheels. He had once had his tail pinched. Willow winced, thinking about Anna's foot.

Once she had shaken the sand and dirt from the ground cloth and folded it, she carried the kitchen crate to the back of the wagon and lifted it, using her thigh as well as all the strength in her arms to hoist it upward. They packed the box very tightly, and the cast iron pots were heavy. The crates they used to sit upon went in last, stacked, with the folded red canvas ground cloth and the kitchen box set down between them.

"Willow?" Anna had pulled herself into a sitting position again. Willow leaned in to see her better.

"What?"

"I can't eat any more."

Willow stepped up into the wagon. "I'll take the dish. How is your—did Fancy—"

"It's no worse," Anna said quickly.

Willow nodded, feeling her eyes sting with tears. She turned to hide them from Anna. What was wrong with her? "I'd better get this one cleaned. I forgot about it," she said, moving toward the back of the wagon, trying to keep the tremble out of her voice. The last thing that Anna needed was a weepy, pitiful sister.

Willow glanced toward the front of the wagon

as she bent over to scoop up some good sand to clean Anna's plate.

"Hey, up. Hey, up." Mr. Hansen was backing the lead yoke of oxen into place. He held the black near-side ox by the strap that ran through her nose ring. Levin was helping him, steadying the off-side ox, a big dun-colored animal they called Dolly.

The banging of the wagon gate made Willow turn. Jordan was taking bundles and sacks, some of which she had just repacked, from the rear of the wagon. She saw the mules, all six of them, tethered together, tied nose-to-tail, their packsaddles already in place.

Mr. Hansen was going to use the mules today, then, to lighten the load on the oxen while the roads were still soft from the rains. Since packing a light load was a lot easier on the mules than pulling the wagon, they would get an easier day, too.

Mr. Hansen had chosen to drive a lighter wagon than many people had, and as a result their teams didn't have to work as hard. And he had insisted, from the beginning, that they leave almost everything behind.

Mr. Hansen had owned a farm near the river crossing that killed Willow's father. As they had waited out the autumn and winter after Willow's father had drowned, trying to sort out what to do next, Mr. Hansen had talked endlessly to her mother about the westward journey, about his own plans to go to California. He had not only read all the guidebooks he could find, he had talked to everyone who had a friend, a neighbor, a cousin who had gone.

As Willow filled in the fire pit, a small ruckus broke out a few wagons down. Two men shouted at each other, standing toe to toe. Willow recognized Mr. Snyder immediately. It took a few seconds for her to realize that the other man was Mr. Gaufer, the train captain. Mr. Snyder often complained; everyone was tired of hearing him. There was too much noise as the camp was being torn down for her to hear what it was about this time. Then she caught the single word "piano" and knew.

This was an old argument, one that had started back in Indiana and would continue until they reached California with, or without, Mr. Snyder's piano—or, rather, his *wife's* piano. Mrs. Snyder loved to play her piano in camp. She played quite well. It was her singing that everyone had come to dread. Gossips said that Mr. Snyder had had to promise his wife he'd bring her piano, or she wouldn't come west with him. The other men thought him soft and silly to give in to such a demand. The women were coming to agree with their men.

The two men were really shouting now. Fancy whined, and Willow looked to see that he was watching them, too. When she cautioned him to keep quiet, Fancy put his head back on his paws. Willow looked back at Jordan. He had the first three mules loaded and was working on the fourth. They all stood patiently, their heads down, their eyes nearly closed.

The shouting went up a notch, and Willow turned back to see Mr. Gaufer and Mr. Snyder standing with their shoulders squared and their heads high. They looked like two men who were about to start fighting, but Willow didn't think it would come to that. Mr. Gaufer had been elected captain because he was capable and because he was even tempered and slow to panic or anger. Willow could hear what they were saying now. Everyone could. The noise had fallen into silence as people stopped what they were doing to hear better.

"You fall behind," Mr. Gaufer was saying. "You sink in sand, you need help with drag coming down steep hills and help going up. The hills are only going to get steeper, Mr. Snyder. I want to cross this river today without having to think about how we are going to get the damn thing across."

Willow nodded. At the last crossing, it had taken an hour just for the piano. Mrs. Snyder seemed to expect everyone to cheerfully help her haul her piano across the prairie, no matter what the cost in time and effort, simply because it was important to her.

"Willow, don't stare!" Willow turned to see her mother scowling. "How I wish they had left it in Indiana!"

Willow nodded and leaned close. "Everyone does, Mama."

"At least someone would have use of it. Or they could have left it at that church in Independence. As it is, they will eventually have to abandon it on the trail and then it will just be ruined. Unless the coyotes learn to play."

Willow smiled again. "Or the Indians."

This time her mother laughed quietly. "They probably would if they had enough chance. Remember the woman who wanted my scissors? How clever she was?"

The argument stopped suddenly. The sky was getting lighter. Dawn was not far off. The camp, a little embarrassed to have been caught listening, went on about its work. Both men glanced around, apparently only then aware of the attention they had attracted. Mr. Gaufer stalked away, leaving Mr. Snyder standing alone.

"Willow?" It was Mr. Hansen. "Help Jordan if

you've nothing of your own left to do. Or Levin. He's sealing up the water barrels and checking the wheels for grease."

Willow's mother nodded and smiled once more. "We'd best both get to work. I just want to get across the river today and leave it behind us."

Willow looked away, but her mother reached out to cup her chin in her hand, turning her back until their eyes met. "I know how it scares you. Be brave, Willow."

"Hey! Help me out, Willow?" This time it was Jordan, and Willow looked, then ran toward him, just in time to keep a flour sack from sliding to the ground.

Jordan wrestled with it. "Hold Lucky steady, will you? The mules were all half asleep until the yelling started. Now they think something is wrong."

Willow took the halter rope and began stroking the mule's soft muzzle. His long ears flickered back and forth. "Easy now. Easy. They've finished now. It's all over, Lucky." The mule lowered his head so that she could rub beneath the leather bands of his halter.

"I doubt it," Jordan said. "I think we are going to have to hear about that piano again real soon."

"I don't understand why they think they are different from everyone else," Willow said. Others in the train had already left their heavy canned goods and other luxuries lying in the weeds along the trail. What would happen to the Snyders when they crossed the deserts, once the mules and oxen were weaker, and grazing was impossible to find? Would they refuse to leave the piano behind then? If so, they might find themselves being left behind as well.

"Ready, here!" Mr. Campbell sang out. No one echoed him. The Campbells were often the first wagon ready, but they always sat patiently while their neighbors finished loading.

Fancy stood and stretched, lowering his chest almost to the ground, his paws extended in front of him. He yawned, then straightened and came close to press himself against Willow's leg. She reached down to pat him, and he licked her hand.

People around the circle began climbing up on the hard wooden drivers' benches. Most just sat quietly. Willow liked this little bit of waiting time when there was nothing to do.

Willow would walk most of the day, looking for firewood or buffalo chips for the evening cookfire. Jordan would look, too, walking alongside the mules to make sure their saddles stayed tight and that nothing fell from their packsaddles to be run over and ruined by the wagons behind them. Levin would probably end up herding stock. Anna would be confined to the makeshift bed again today, and their mother would ride on the driver's bench next to Mr. Hansen.

"Ready, Willow?" her mother called from the wagon seat. "Give your brothers a hand if they need it."

Willow nodded. "I will."

"I'm set!" Jordan called.

Then they were all silent. It was like a pot starting to boil. Every person who finished with preparations stood waiting, increasing the pressure a little. No one said anything, not even Mr. Gaufer. The silence thickened, and even the animals seemed to quiet themselves.

Some people were looking back toward the road the wagon train had traveled the day before, others were squinting ahead. Everyone knew that there were awful hardships and sorrows lurking along it. The shallow graves were there almost every day to remind them, just in case they should forget. But California lay somewhere at the end of that same road.

Suddenly the wagons started to roll. Without a signal, the wheels creaked as they began to turn, as if pushed by the urgency of the families loaded in them. A few seconds later, the sun sparkled, a fire burning just below the edge of the horizon.

CHAPTER FIVE

Willow's family ended up about a third of the way back in the train. This was Willow's favorite position. She felt safer than she did when they were at one end or the other. And today, since there had been rain, it was even better than usual. On dry days they all wore kerchiefs over their noses and mouths to thin the choking dust.

This morning, the air was rainwashed, and the prairie smelled of damp sod and early sun. It would be hot later, but for now, it was pleasant, and Willow tried to enjoy it. She walked off to one side of the wagons, Fancy at her heels. Jordan strode along beside the lead mule, the lead rope loose in one hand. Levin walked on the other side, picking up rocks to throw, making target practice out of everything that moved. A few days before he had killed a grouse, and their mother had added it to the stew that night.

As the sun cleared the edge of the world and the first rays of light streaked across the land, Willow retied her bonnet, then picked Fancy up and kissed his woolly head. He wriggled to lick her face, then struggled to get down. This early in the day he preferred to walk on his own.

The road had firmed up quite a bit from the day before, though it was still muddy. The oxen plodded along, the wet soil squelching up through their big, cloven hooves with every slow, heavy step. Their massive heads swung a little from side to side with the pendulum cadence of their walk.

After a while, Willow walked close enough to Jordan to talk. Fancy stayed at her heels. The mules looked at him askance once or twice, then ignored him. In spite of what Mr. Hansen thought, Fancy was really very well behaved around stock. He almost never barked, and he made his soft, high whining sounds only when he was trying to tell her something.

"You know what I want to do when we get to

California?" Jordan asked as soon as she fell in beside him.

This was one of Anna and Jordan's favorite games because it passed the time. Jordan was fifteen, and Willow was always amazed at how much he still enjoyed the games they had all played when they were younger. Levin, at sixteen, would not play anymore, not even with Anna.

Jordan drew in a big breath. "I am going to eat apricots and apples and alum and ants and aster flowers and . . ." he trailed off, unable to think of anything else that started with an "a."

"I am going to eat beets and baked biscuits and butter and barley and bitters and black walnuts." Willow said the last two words with a flourish and then stopped instead of faltering while she was trying to think of just one more. She thought it sounded better that way, as if she had meant to quit, not that she had run out of "b" words.

"I miss Anna," Jordan said suddenly. He lifted his chin and gestured toward the wagon, rolling slowly along twenty or thirty feet in front of them. Little bits of mud and grass clung to the iron wheel rims.

"I do, too," Willow admitted.

"You think she's going to be all right?"

Willow nodded, then shook her head. "I don't know. I did at first, but it looks as bad as it did that first night. Worse even. It's swollen huge, Jordan."

He nodded. "Mama says she will heal. But you know Mama."

Willow nodded, understanding him perfectly. Their mother was the kind of person who refused to admit it was raining until the drops rolled down her cheeks and dripped beneath her collar.

Thinking about rain made Willow wonder if the cloud bank to the west had thinned or thickened. She walked a little faster, angling away from Jordan, until she could see past the wagons. Her spirits fell a little. The cloud bank had thickened. She squinted. Or was she imagining it? "The worst thing today would be more rain," she called back to Jordan.

"The worst thing would be if Anna gets to where she can't travel for a while," he answered her.

Willow felt a shock go through her heart, and she turned to look at him. He nodded, a grim expression on his face. It was something that Willow had never thought about. What would they do? Stay behind while the other wagons went on? It hadn't happened in their train yet, but everyone had heard the stories. Once a wagon was off by itself, the Indians weren't as afraid to come and ask for food or clothing. Or to do harm. And once people were separated on the journey, there was a chance they would never rejoin. There were so many cut-offs and shortcuts and decisions to make about where, exactly, to settle once the West was finally reached. Willow had heard Mrs. Banner describe a friend of hers who had gotten separated from her son and daughter-in-law. It had taken three years for her to find out where they had ended up and that they were safe.

"I hope we make it before snow, at least," Jordan said.

Willow nodded and swallowed hard. "You're full of gloom today, Jordan."

He glanced at her. "Rain is bad enough. What will it be like if we're still traveling when it snows?"

"We'll be all right," Willow said automatically.

"You sound like Mother."

"Mr. Hansen says it, too."

Jordan shrugged. "We got a late start from St. Louis, though. What with the Holcombs' baby and—"

"She delayed us exactly one day, Jordan Chase. Her husband wouldn't allow her any more than that, remember? You can't hold poor Mrs. Holcomb accountable for what was mostly the Banners' fault."

Jordan glanced back over his shoulder. "Not so loud."

Willow put her hand over her mouth. She wasn't sure why she had reacted to quickly. Maybe it was all the talk about snow and Anna's getting sicker that had made her jumpy. The Banners *had* been the ones to hold up the train, though. They had had to wait for Mrs. Banner's uncle to arrive. He was traveling with them and was putting up a third of the provisions money. Without him, they couldn't have come at all.

Then, just after Mrs. Banner's uncle had arrived, the preacher had one yoke of oxen die for no reason anyone could ever figure out. It had taken him almost a week to find a good replacement team. The delays had somehow added up until late April, so they had left nearly a month after they'd meant to.

Willow glanced at Jordan. He was lost in his own thoughts, too. And as she watched him, she saw him lengthen his step a little, pick up the mule's pace. Not only was everyone conscious of hurrying to avoid cold weather, the grass had been significantly reduced by wagon trains that got off on time.

Willow gave up on Jordan remembering their game. She was content to walk with him in silence. Fancy trotted at her heels. He looked up and gave her a dog's grin, his tongue lolling to one side.

Looking down at Fancy, Willow noticed the

ground beneath her feet. There was no grass at all here. The little there had been was flattened by the rains. She stared, startled by an odd odor in the air, like bruised lettuce leaves.

"Hail," Jordan said, at the same instant she thought it. "Big hail."

Willow nodded. Every stem of grass had been beaten flat, as though it had rained hammers instead of water. She pointed when she saw a bush that had nearly half its leaves in a spatter around its base. "I'm glad it missed us."

Jordan shrugged. "It's fun to have throw fights with. Stings more than a snowball."

Willow laughed. "You just like it because you can always beat Levin. You've always been the better aim. If you got a game going with the Campbell boys, they'd pound you."

Jordan raised his head. "Which is exactly why I don't. There is nothing wrong with choosing your adversary, is there?"

Willow shook her head, laughing. "No."

Fancy barked sharply. This was his warning voice and Willow looked ahead again. She caught her breath and pointed. Along the crest of the rise they were approaching she could see silhouettes: men mounted on wiry horses. They wore no hats and their dark hair streamed out behind them. Indians.

Willow heard the murmur run through the train, working its way from the front to the back. They hadn't had trouble yet, but no one ever seemed to know which Indians were friendly and which might not be. Up and down the lines of wagons, Willow heard men's voices and here and there a clattering of metal. The men were getting their guns close to hand. She saw Mr. Hansen reach beneath the seat, then lay his rifle across his knees.

Willow slowed her step as the wagons, one by one, came to a halt. Her heart thudding, she went to stand by Jordan.

"They probably just want food or calico or something," Jordan said.

Willow didn't answer. She had heard many stories about Indians—but so far she had never seen one who wasn't friendly. In fact, they were almost too friendly. They didn't seem to realize that they startled people, just walking up out of the bushes, peering into people's wagons. This morning there were five Indians. Willow counted twice. Five that she could see, anyway.

"You're shaking like a leaf in the wind," Jordan whispered. "They scare me," Willow whispered back. Three or four of the Indians had dismounted now. Their hair was long, almost to their waists, shining blue black in the slanting, early sunshine.

Mr. Gaufer was talking to them. He was using the broad gestures people called "Indian signs." Willow always wondered if anyone really understood what was being said. She could hear the Indians speaking a little, too. Some of the Indians they had met spoke a few words of English. After all, they had been seeing wagon-train travelers—and often trading with them—for years.

One of the braves walked briskly down the line of wagons. He looked into the faces of the people he passed, finally stopping at the preacher's wagon, three wagons away. He stood without speaking, staring at the preacher and his wife. Fancy yapped, and Willow saw one of the braves glance in her direction. Fancy growled protectively. Willow scooped Fancy up and the Indian turned away.

"What's he *doing*?" Willow breathed.

Jordan shrugged. "I can't tell."

Willow looked back at the group of Indians at the head of the wagon train. Mr. Campbell was talking to them now. Willow saw him proffer a bolt of bright red calico cloth to the tall man who seemed to be the Indians' leader.

Willow held her breath. They had brought calico especially for trading. They had beads, too, and cheap steel knives and little mirrors. She watched, hoping the Indians would be satisfied and leave, but they did not make a move to go as the leader accepted the calico and gestured elaborately. He was talking loudly at the same time, and his voice sounded angry.

Willow glanced nervously at the Indian who had come down the line of wagons. He was saying something to the preacher now, his voice insistent, the word at first unintelligible to Willow. Then, suddenly, she could understand him.

"Medicine?"

The preacher shook his head, and Willow knew he was trying to indicate that he and his wife, out of all the wagons in the line, were least likely to have what the brave wanted. Families with children usually brought a larger assortment of remedies.

The Indian shrugged and tried again. "Medicine? Boy sick."

Willow bit her lip, glancing back and forth between the brave who stood so close—only thirty or so feet away from her now—and the group of Indians at the head of the train.

"Medicine," the Indian said again, and the preacher shook his head.

"We don't have much. Almost nothing. Not enough for ourselves, even," he said, angling his body so that he sat half turned away from the Indian. The Indian made a face of disgust and walked to the next wagon. He stared at the

Wallaces, a young couple still both in their teens. "Medicine?" The Indian gestured toward their wagon. Ben Wallace shook his head.

"No. Not to trade."

The Indian walked again, this time stopping only briefly at the next wagon to ask his question and get a negative shake of the head. Willow watched.

"No one wants to give him anything." She said it so quietly that only Jordan could hear her.

He nodded and answered from the side of his mouth. "Can't blame them."

"They call themselves Christians, Jordan. They all do. Especially the preacher." She saw the Indian skip the next wagon, then stop to stare at her mother. Levin came to stand closer to the wagon, straight and stiff as he stared at the Indian. Jordan took a step forward, too. The Indian met Levin's gaze for a moment, then Jordan's. Then he looked back at their mother.

"Medicine?"

Willow couldn't see her mother's face. Or Mr. Hansen's. She could see Mr. Hansen lift the rifle a little, though. He did not point it at the Indian, but he held it ready. Fancy wriggled and Willow flinched, startled to find him still in her arms. She put her hand around his muzzle. "Be quiet."

Mr. Hansen leaned out around the wagon bench to give Willow and Fancy a hard look. Willow could read his thoughts from his stern face. *Keep hold of that dog.*

Fancy struggled to get her hand off his muzzle, and she tightened her grip, speaking very quietly into his ear. He settled in her arms. From where she stood, a little to one side of the wagon, Willow could see her mother turn to crawl back through the opening in the canvas cover. She was back in a few moments, a box in her hands. Willow recognized it. It was their remedy box, packed carefully with cod-liver oil, quinine, laudanum, blue mass, sassafras, ginger root, and a bottle of Dr. Sneller's Pain Reliever for Teeth and Gums.

"Your boy is sick?" Willow was startled by the steadiness of her mother's voice as she opened the box.

The brave nodded somberly.

"Fever?" Willow's mother asked.

The Indian tilted his head but did not answer. Willow's mother tried again. She pressed her hand to her forehead, then jerked it back as though it had gotten burned. "Hot," she said distinctly. Then she shuddered, miming an attack of shivering ague. She sat straight again. "Fever?" She touched her forehead again. "Hot?"

The Indian, in two quick steps, climbed up

the step and leaned across a startled Mr. Hansen to touch Willow's mother's forehead. "Hot," he agreed. Then he began to tremble, his whole body shaking in a very good imitation of someone with ague. He leapt back off the wagon step. "Boy sick," he repeated, and waited. Mr. Hansen sat rigidly, the rifle held in white-knuckled hands.

Willow watched her mother take out one of the little blue bottles of quinine. The Indian looked at her gravely and raised his hand to take the little bottle from her. "Good," he said, looking right into her eyes. He held her gaze so long that Mr. Hansen shifted on the seat, raising the gun a little higher and swinging the barrel vaguely toward the Indian.

"You are very welcome," Willow heard her mother say politely. "I will hope and pray that your son gets well." She pantomimed taking a tiny sip from the bottle. "Not too much. A little." She held up three fingers, then took three sips of air, raising an imaginary bottle.

The Indian nodded as though he had understood. He climbed down and faced Willow and Jordan for a second. Fancy twisted in Willow's grasp. Knowing he would bark if the Indian approached her, Willow tightened her grip on his muzzle. The Indian stared for a second or two longer, then turned and walked back toward the front of the wagon train. He didn't look right or left now that he had what he wanted. He walked like a deer, Willow thought, faster than you thought from watching the effortless and graceful gait. In seconds he was back beside his pony, swinging up in a single, fluid motion.

He turned his mount and cantered away without a word to his companions. A few minutes later, the rest of them were gone, too, carrying two bolts of cloth and three mirrors. Mr. Gaufer gave the signal, and the wagons eased back into motion. Levin walked close to the wagon bench. Willow saw him glancing up at their mother with plain admiration on his face. She felt the same way. If it had been her, she'd have been shaking and nervous.

Conversation began to swell again as the Indians rode back to the top of the ridge at a full gallop and disappeared over it. Willow released Fancy and he shook himself, whining a little to let her know he would have protected her. "I'm sorry I had to hold you so hard," Willow said. "I really am, Fancy. But who knows what they would do to you if you went running up to them barking? They might just kill you so they wouldn't have to listen to you. People say the most awful things about Indians."

"They probably aren't anything to worry about yet," Jordan said evenly, and Willow knew he was trying to impress her with his calmness. "It's only once we get farther west that there's been much trouble."

"I've read the same books you have," Willow told him impatiently. "I think that, by then, people are sick of having to trade with them all the time, annoyed with having them just appear like that, scaring everyone. So they shoot at the Indians and the trouble starts."

"I admit it's strange the way they come up out of nowhere," Jordan said, pushing his hair back out of his eyes. "And hard to keep your nerve. You just be careful with Fancy when they're around. He'd jump at a bear if he thought you needed help."

Willow nodded. "I'll be careful."

"That was foolish," Willow heard Mr. Hansen say. She strained but could not hear her mother's answer. Willow felt like telling Mr. Hansen to be quiet. If her mother hadn't given the Indian some quinine, he could still be here, waiting for trouble to start.

"I don't ever want you speaking out like that again. I will do the talking." Willow saw her mother stiffen, and she made another low answer. "It's dangerous," Mr. Hansen went on. "Now that they've noticed you . . . women have been kidnapped, you know."

"I was only being kind," Willow heard her mother say, very clearly. Mr. Hansen nodded curtly, glancing around. Willow turned her head so he wouldn't realize she had heard. When he spoke next, he dropped his voice so that she could not understand any more of what he said.

Willow looked sidelong at Jordan's face. If he heard the argument going on at the front of the wagon, he gave no sign of it. Willow wondered if Anna had heard what their mother had said. Probably, if she wasn't asleep or too sick with her pain. Willow swept Fancy up off the ground and hugged him. Startled, he yelped, drawing a hard look from Mr. Hansen, and she set him down. He trotted along at her feet, his muzzle still high, scenting the Indians as they passed over the part of the road where the main party had stood.

"Look," Jordan said abruptly, pointing.

Willow turned to her right to follow his gesture. The storm clouds along the western horizon had accumulated like steam under the blue saucer of the sky. They were no longer fleecy white. Their bellies were swelling, darkening into the color of rain, gray and dreary. As Willow watched, she saw a tiny, distant sparkle of lightning.

CHAPTER SIX

As the excitement of the Indians' visit faded, everyone began to notice the cloudline darkening. Willow could feel the uneasiness in the people around her swelling, hear it in the curses of the men as they prodded the hungry oxen into hurrying. As far ahead as she could see, the already sparse grass on both sides of the rutted road was bruised flat, muddied. Had the hail ruined the grass for another half mile or another ten miles? There was no way to know.

They had not been in sight of the South Platte River since they had started that morning—sometimes the wheel-rut road curved away from it for a few miles. But the roar of the river, less than a quarter mile away to the west, let them know that the waters hadn't yet abated. If it rained again and they couldn't cross for a few more days, what would the animals eat? How many more oxen and cattle would they lose before they managed to get to better pastures?

Willow saw Mr. Hansen beckon to Levin. Levin stopped his rock-throwing practice and trotted close to the wagon. Mr. Hansen reached beneath the seat, then leaned out to hand Levin the Colt pistol. Levin nodded smartly at whatever Mr. Hansen was saying to him, then he started walking, headed against the current of people and wagons, making his way toward the back of the train.

"Is he worried about the Indians stealing stock?" Jordan asked as Levin came past.

Levin pushed the pistol through his belt and shook his head. "He didn't say that. He said he wanted to make sure there were enough hands back there in case the lightning came closer and spooked the herd into stampede."

Jordan arched his brows. "You're supposed to shoot at the clouds if they dare to come this way?"

Levin shrugged. "He probably didn't want to worry Mama about it more than he had to."

"Levin!"

Mr. Hansen's shout made Willow look up. Levin stepped around them without another word, taking long strides, angling off to the side to clear the caravan. Willow saw Mr. Hansen glaring at her and Jordan once Levin had gone, but she refused to bow her head or look away. They had cost Levin about three whole seconds. That was all. He would not have tarried to talk more than another moment, either. They were not stupid. They didn't want to have the beef cattle stolen any more than Mr. Hansen did. After all, they would starve right along with him, wouldn't they?

Mr. Hansen still had not turned back to face the road. But he was looking past her now, she realized. He frowned and jabbed a finger, pointing. Willow turned in time to see what was wrong. Fancy had followed Levin. Willow whistled.

"Go back. You can't come with me now," Levin scolded loudly, pausing in his stride long enough for Willow to whistle. Fancy came bounding back. Willow walked along, stealing glances at the wagon bench while she chided Fancy. Mr. Hansen finally faced front again. Willow saw her mother say something to him, resting her hand lightly on his arm for a moment. Willow set Fancy down again and walked along with her head high. She *was* embarrassed by her own carelessness. But Mr. Hansen did not have to know it.

Willow had to lengthen her stride and walk a little faster than usual to keep up. Urgency and worry were in the air again. The drivers were pushing the oxen along now.

"We'll likely stop at noon if there's any grazing along here," Jordan said and Willow shot him a grateful look for breaking the silence.

"Do you think the Indians will come back?"

Jordan shook his head and pointed at the Campbell boys walking toward the rear, carrying rifles. "If they do, they'll find half the rifles in the train back there. I don't think they will. Not today anyway. Why would they warn us by showing themselves, then attack? If they want the horses, they'll come at night. If they want to kill us, we'll never know they are there until they . . ." He trailed off and tugged at his own hair.

Willow shuddered. "The thought of someone being scalped makes me feel sick."

"Makes everybody sick. That's why they do it, I think. Scares people." Jordan reached back to tug at a saddle strap on the lead mule. "But who knows why they do anything? We can't talk to them well enough."

Willow shook her head to get her hair back off

her forehead. Her bonnet was loose, and she tightened the strings. "I wonder if they hate us all."

Jordan shrugged. "They must. Why else would they steal from the farms and wagon trains so often?" He paused. Willow knew he was restraining himself; he knew talk about Indians and their cruelties upset her.

"And I know they do even worse than steal," she added finally.

He nodded. "But I think if they are treated fair, they can be good neighbors."

"I hope so," Willow answered. All the way across Kansas Territory they had heard the settlers complain about the Indians walking right into their sod houses and dugouts, looking around with curiosity. They had also heard stories of the Indians' somber dignity and their help in times of need. But there were just as many accounts of murder and cruelty and torture. How was a person supposed to know which kind of Indian was which? Or were they all capable of helping or hurting and moved only by whim? Willow shivered, remembering her grandfather's stories of France, the hangings and the poor children starving while the rich passed by in carriages laughing. Why should Indians be less cruel?

Jordan was checking the mules' saddles,

watching their gait, making the little adjustments that would prevent bruised backs or rubbed hair that would then become saddle sores on their backs and withers.

"Willow?"

The voice from the wagon was faint. Willow did not hesitate. She hurried forward, walking along just behind the wagon gate. "Yes, Anna?"

"Is there water?"

"I'll get it." Willow crossed to the far side of the moving wagon, keeping an eye on Fancy. The drinking cup hung from an oiled flax cord bound to a peg set into the side board. She slipped the cup free, then uncorked the cask and filled the little cup. It was muddy. The dirt couldn't settle while the wagons were moving, bumping along the road like this. They had refilled the water barrels at the Platte River. Willow stared at the water, almost overcome with homesickness for a few seconds. She missed clean sheets, clean water, a clean kitchen, and food without grit in it. She missed feeling safe and sleeping soundly. She missed her cousins and her friends and her *home*.

With all her will, Willow forced the homesickness down. It would hardly matter if she cried, would it? What would change? And Anna needed a drink of water.

Willow called Fancy as she crossed back behind the wagon again. He danced along behind her, making a wide arc around the wheels. He had learned his lesson.

"You stay close, Fancy. You just follow the wagon," she said sternly as she gathered her skirts.

"I'll watch him," Jordan called, and Willow smiled her thanks. One hand full of calico and the other balancing the cup, she timed the step up perfectly, released her skirts, and grabbed the wagon gate as she swung one leg over. She ducked beneath the circle of gathered canvas, coming up from under the cloth like a child playing peekaboo in a curtain, the water cup held firmly in one extended hand.

The stifling interior of the wagon smelled musty. If they couldn't get their clothes and the tents out soon and dry them, everything would mildew. In the middle of the wagon, lying on her plank bed, Anna had propped herself up on both elbows.

"Thank you, Willow. I could have called to Mama, but I thought Mr. Hansen might make us stop, and then we'd lose our place, and—" She gestured to the front of the wagon. The heavy, oiled canvas cover behind the driver's bench had been drawn across the opening, no doubt to keep drafts from reaching Anna. Willow smiled to reassure her sister.

"I don't mind a bit, Anna." She steadied herself against the sudden rise and fall of the wagon as the wheels went over a rut. "Call me for anything if you need to. I would ride back here with you except—"

"Oh, I know," Anna said quickly. "I'm trying to get used to it. I just wish Mama wouldn't close it all up so tight."

Willow glanced back at the cinched canvas cover. "I'll let it out a little when I get down." She made her way forward with the cup, letting her arm absorb the worst of the bumps and jolts so that only a little spilled.

Anna took the cup. This close, Willow could see how pale she was. A film of sweat made her face shine a little, even in the dim light. "What happened? Tell me about it."

"Finish your water and let me help you lie back first."

Anna drank the cloudy water without any comment at all. Willow took the cup and held it loosely in her lap as she described the Indian men to her sister. "And the one who talked to Mama wanted medicine—or at least that's what she gave him. He had a child with fever and shakes."

Anna eyes widened. "He *said* that?"

Willow shook her head. "He acted it out and Mama understood him. She gave him a bottle of quinine." Willow leaned forward to whisper. "Could you hear? What did Mr. Hansen say to her afterward?"

Anna beckoned her closer. Once her lips were almost on Willow's ear, she whispered. "He said she was a fool and could have endangered all of us. Now I understand what he meant. But he's wrong, don't you think?"

Willow nodded. "I do. If we are cruel and unfriendly to them, they will only hate us more. Jordan said as much, too. Mama is good-hearted." She frowned. "Sometimes I hate him."

Anna looked startled. She beckoned Willow to lean close again. "Don't say that, Willow. It's wicked. He's our stepfather, after all."

Willow sat back a little but kept her voice very low. "Well, I do. I am sick of hearing him tell all of us how foolish we are." Anna's eyes widened, but Willow wasn't afraid of being overheard. The wagon train was a constant jumble of noises and besides, she had kept her voice just barely above a whisper.

Anna struggled to prop herself up again. "Are we going to cross the river today? What are people saying?"

Willow shook her head, her stomach constricting. "I don't know. There are rain clouds west of us, and the river is still high—you can hear it."

"Have we passed good grass yet?"

Willow shook her head, pitying Anna. It had to be awful to lie here wondering what was going on. "No grass, and there was a hailstorm all through here. What little there was is ruined."

Anna was silent. There was a long pause and Willow fought the urge to leave. Anna had to be really lonely and miserable, but it was hard not to feel sick from the steamy, swaying interior.

"Is my foot turning black, Willow?" Anna asked suddenly, her eyes searching. "You look at it when Mama changes the bandage. She won't let me. What does it look like?"

Willow forced herself to smile. "It looks better and better, Anna." She swallowed. "It's still quite swollen, but it will heal. It hasn't turned dark or anything. Of course it will heal."

Anna's eyes brimmed with tears, and Willow pretended not to notice. It would do them very little good to cry together, and that was what was about to happen. She reined in her own feelings and stood up, brushing at her skirt. "I could bring you more water."

Anna shook her head politely, wiping her eyes. Her voice was firm. "Perhaps in an hour or so,

Willow." She handed Willow the empty cup.

"I'll listen for your call, Anna. I'll be close." Willow was trying hard to hide how much she wanted to be out in the sunshine. She looked at the lanterns swinging from the arched bows that held up the canvas roof. Her stomach clenched, and she had to look down again. "I had better go see what Fancy is up to. I left him with Jordan."

"Where's Levin?" Anna asked suddenly. "I thought I heard his voice up with Mama and Mr. Hansen."

The motion of the wagon was almost more than Willow could stand, but she stood still and looked at her sister. "Mr. Hansen sent him back to keep an eye on the stock with all the others."

Anna nodded. "Because of the Indians?"

Willow shrugged, desperate to go, and determined not to say anything to upset Anna. "I think so. But Jordan says that's silly. Why would they show themselves, then attack when we are ready for them?"

Anna relaxed visibly. Willow was ashamed of her selfishness and glad she had stayed long enough to reassure her younger sister. Of course Anna was even more uneasy than she normally would have been. Anna couldn't help fight, couldn't shoot, couldn't hide, couldn't *run*.

"Well . . ." Anna smiled but a jolting bump turned it into grimace of pain. Once she had recovered herself, she finished. "Willow? On your way, please make some room for air to come in?"

"Yes. I'll come see you after a while, Anna. Try to rest."

Anna nodded and Willow turned, making her way to the rear of the wagon. She loosened the cord that gathered the canvas into a puckered rosette until a circle of sun appeared in the center. She looked back and saw Anna smile, then climbed out, perching on the back step. She stood still, riding the rise and fall of one more bump. Then, gathering her skirts, she jumped backward, landing reasonably gracefully.

Willow pulled in three or four big breaths to clear the damp, mildew odor of the wagon from her lungs. She said a silent, quick prayer that they could sleep outside tonight, that the rain would stop—and immediately felt guilty. If she were going to pray, it should be for their safety or Anna's recovery.

"Willow, call Fancy," Jordan shouted.

Willow turned and whistled. Fancy ran toward her, and she could tell from the way he gathered himself that he was about to leap. She steadied herself and caught him midair. He wriggled against her, welcoming her back into the sunshine. Jordan was fussing with one of the mule's bridles, loosening a throat latch or tightening it; Willow couldn't tell. The mule kept walking; nothing bothered the mules, short of a rattlesnake or a downpour.

"He wants to jump up like that all the time, Willow," Jordan complained. "He's gotten too used to your carrying him."

"I only started because his paws were raw for those first few weeks," Willow defended herself. "And besides—"

"He's yours. He's bound to be troublesome."

Willow started to say something back, but then she saw him holding back a grin. She pushed at his shoulder and he laughed. Then his face became serious. "How is Anna?"

Willow took another deep breath. "All right, I think, Jordan."

Jordan finished with the strap, then faced her again. "The Williamses' baby died."

Willow caught her breath. "But he seemed so healthy. And it's been nearly two weeks since he was born."

Jordan shrugged. "Tom just told me, walking past. He was on his way back to help guard the stock. He says his Pa wants to stop long enough at noon so they can bury the baby. His mother is not too well, either."

Willow glanced involuntarily toward the front of their wagon to where her own mother sat, her belly swelling a little more every day. "His mother is just grieving. You know how hard it is to bury family and know you'll never see the grave again."

Jordan shook his head. "Tom says she's sick, too. Fever."

"Oh." Willow looked at the horizon. The sky seemed endlessly arching, endlessly deep. The string of clouds had become a distant, roiling wall of gray and white. She looked back at her brother, but he had turned to fiddle with the horsehair cinch on the second mule's packsaddle. He was whistling softly, an old hymn that had been their father's favorite.

CHAPTER SEVEN

The rhythm of the walking went on. The sun rolled higher in the sky. Willow kept watching the clouds. They were boiling up against the edge of the blue dome of the sky, no doubt about it. The real question was whether the rain would hit the wagon train or skip over them and fall on some other part of the prairie. If it hit southwest, upstream, that would be bad. If the river rose any more, they'd be stuck on this side even longer. How many days could the oxen last, working this hard without food? Homesickness hit Willow again, and she sighed.

"Do you ever wish we had gone back home

after Pa died?" Willow asked Jordan.

He looked up, startled at her voice. "Willow, this is the easy half." He laughed wryly, then shrugged. "Sometimes I think about the desert crossing after South Pass, and I can't sleep." Then he raised his eyes. "We'll make it, Willow. Mr. Gaufer is smart, and we are all strong and healthy."

Willow heard the distant growl of thunder and looked toward the clouds. They were still far west, but they filled about a quarter of the sky now. Winks of lightning flashed inside them.

"Rest stop!"

The call came down the line. One by one the wagons halted, each driver careful to leave a little distance between his wagon and the next. Willow turned to pick up Fancy. She waited, wondering what was going on. They often rested ten minutes out of every hour once it was hot, but it was still cool. Maybe they had found a place to cross? Or maybe they had seen Indians again? Willow saw Mr. Hansen climb down stiffly. He helped her mother alight, then immediately walked around the oxen, checking their harness for burrs or loose tacks, slipped straps or uneven yokes. He did this every time the teams were stopped, for any reason, unless some emergency claimed his attention.

Willow's mother walked heavily to the rear of

the wagon and climbed up. Her movements were slow, precise. After the bumping of the wagon, the ground always felt a little too still, too solid. Willow could hear her talking to Anna. A moment later, she was climbing back down, half turning so that she could see the footstep around her pregnant belly.

"Help me get the linens out for a little sun, Willow," she called, without looking up.

Willow set Fancy down, whistling at him to keep him beside her as she joined her mother at the back of the wagon.

Willow glanced up. "Do you feel sick, Mama?"

Her mother shook her head. "A little tired some days. I will be just fine."

From the carefully cheerful, even tone of her voice, Willow knew someone had already told her about the Williamses' baby.

Shouting from the head of the train brought them both around to stand side by side, listening. Jordan, who had been switching the heavier loads to the mules that still seemed freshest, stopped what he was doing, too.

"Can you see anything?" Willow's mother asked. "Is Mr. Snyder involved?"

Willow squinted, straining to see or hear, but beyond the fact that men were still shouting, she couldn't see anything.

"Jordan?" Willow's mother turned, her hands pressed against her abdomen.

"Mama?" He looked up from his mules.

"Go see what the shouting is about, please. Then hurry back."

Jordan strode away, and Willow whistled to keep Fancy from following him.

"Get out some hard bread, Willow. I want to see if I can catch someone headed to the back. Levin will be hungry by now."

"I'll take him bread, Mama," Willow said quickly. She was so used to walking that a half mile or so added onto the day was nothing—and she liked to see the other families on the way. In some ways, a short rest stop was more relaxed than a noon dinner stop or a night camp. There wasn't enough time to do laundry or cook or much else, really. So people could chat a little bit.

"I want you to go visit with Anna, please. Do what you can to cheer her up, Willow."

Willow glanced at the wagon, imagining how hot it would be inside, how stuffy. "I will, Mama."

Inside the wagon with Anna, while her mother waited for Jordan, Willow tried to be cheerful. It was so hot that Fancy whined, then circled and lay down, panting. Anna was sleepy, too, and not really hungry. She picked at her hard bread, then slid it onto the plank bed beside her, and closed her eyes.

"You need to eat more, Anna."

Without opening her eyes, Anna took a long breath. "I can't."

After a few more silent minutes, Willow realized that Anna had fallen into a heavy sleep. Willow took the bread from her loose fingers and tiptoed out of the wagon, lifting Fancy out with her. Her mother looked at her sharply.

"Doesn't Anna want to talk?"

Willow took a bite of the hard bread and shook her head. "She's asleep."

"She was hardly able to rest last night," Willow's mother said, and Willow could hear the worry in her voice. "Perhaps she can at least nap a bit while we are here. I would ride with her, but I can't stand the swaying back there now." She pressed one hand against her belly for the fleetest instant. "Jordan is coming back, I think. Isn't that Jordan?"

Willow squinted, trying to pick out Jordan's blue shirt and loping walk. "Yes," she said, spotting him. "It is."

"Do you see your stepfather?"

Willow shook her head, recoiling from her mother's pointed use of the word *stepfather*. "No. Not yet, anyway."

Her mother turned toward the river. "Karl told me they were sending out riders to look for a possible ford farther on."

Willow felt a wash of distaste at her mother's intimate use of Mr. Hansen's Christian name. The only other man Willow had ever heard her mother address so familiarly had been her father—and even after all this time, it still bothered her.

A second later, Willow felt the creeping fear that she always struggled with when they crossed a river. As Jordan approached, it stood close behind her, tickling her neck, and chilling her sweaty hands.

"They found a ford," Jordan said from twenty feet away. Fancy ran to meet him and turned to follow at his heels. Jordan kept talking as he approached. "They think it's a good spot. Deep enough that they need a swimmer for the first pass with the cord. I am going to carry it."

Willow saw her mother go pale and knew she was regretting having sent Jordan forward. She fidgeted with her apron, then bent awkwardly to pat Fancy. Jordan pretended not to notice her agitation, but Willow knew he had.

"The argument," Jordan went on when neither his sister or his mother said anything, "was with Snyder, of course. Who else?"

Willow's mother exhaled. "The piano?"

Jordan laughed. "Of course. They have an elaborate plan that will require only three ferry wagons tied together to carry the thing across without getting a drop of water on it."

"They have managed every other ford without that," Willow's mother said indignantly.

Jordan shrugged. "The water is pretty high, Mama. And there's some flood wash coming down, plane-tree branches and mats of willow."

"Then let someone else swim it."

He straightened up, surprised at the quick change of subject, but equal to it, looking more man than boy. "I'm the best. They know it."

Willow watched him. Jordan was the best at more than just swimming. He ran and climbed better than most boys, and he was as strong as any man already. She envied his lack of fear. Without meaning to, she imagined the rush of muddy water and felt her neck prickle.

"I think I'd best eat my hard bread after I swim, Mama," Jordan was saying. "Not before. They are going to take me down there now. It's about a quarter mile more is all. They want to get things set up quick."

Willow glanced up. Mr. Hansen was coming. "Jordan!" he called. "Mr. Gaufer is waiting on you. I'll stay with your mother."

Willow watched her brother kiss their mother's cheek lightly, then turn and head for the front of the wagon train again, settling into his long-strided, loping walk. Willow's mother greeted Mr. Hansen, her voice firmly cheerful. Mr. Hansen gave Willow a quick, here-and-gone smile that might have been her imagination before he took the hard bread her mother offered him. He went to sit on the footstep to eat. Fancy whined a little, apologizing, then left Willow's side to go lie in the shade of the wagon.

After a few minutes, the eldest Campbell boy walked up. "Levin says thanks for the bread, ma'am. They are watering the stock now, so when the time comes they'll swim, not stop to drink."

Willow's mother smiled at him. "I appreciate your carrying the bread to him."

"It was no trouble," he responded politely.

Willow happened to look back toward the end of the wagon train just as the Williams family emerged, in a solemn line, walking slowly away from the train. Mr. Williams was carrying a small bundle. Willow gestured, and her mother turned to look.

"Oh, it's too cruel," she breathed after a moment. "To have to bury a baby here. To have to *hurry*." She jabbed an angry finger at the endless sky overhead, then at the boundless emptiness of the flat land that stretched away to meet it at the horizon. Then she took a deep breath and met Willow's eyes. "We have much to be thankful for, Willow."

Willow nodded, not meaning it. How could she be thankful that her father had drowned? "Should we . . ." she gestured toward the Williams family, making their ragged procession onto the unmarked prairie beyond the road. Mr. Williams began to dig. The ground was soft from the rain.

"If they had wanted us, they would have asked," Willow's mother said.

Without saying a word, Willow reached out and took her mother's hand. For a moment, they simply hung onto each other. Then Willow's mother squeezed her hand and let go, running her palms down the front of her skirt to smooth it. "I suppose we should get started here. May as well be ready."

"We will likely be unloading everything," Mr. Hansen said from the footstep where he sat. "Mr. Gaufer has proposed using three or four of the best-suited wagons to ferry goods, then women and children. The men and boys will swim the stock across. Everyone thought it a good plan except for Mr. Snyder."

"The piano?" Willow's mother asked, as though Jordan had not already told them.

Mr. Hansen nodded curtly. "If there is enough time, and if everyone is not dangerously exhausted, we agreed to help him when his turn comes up."

Willow heard the impatience in his voice and knew that nearly every man, woman, and child on the train shared it. Yet they had to agree to help Mr. Snyder in order to appease him so he would get out of the way and let the rest of them run the business of crossing the river. It was most likely going to be a costly promise, Willow thought. When had they ever forded a river without tiring everyone to the last ounce of endurance?

"Wait until we hear that the lines are across— then we can begin unpacking," Mr. Hansen said. Willow's mother nodded calmly. Willow tried to look brave so that perhaps she could begin to feel brave, but her fear embraced her again. She knew that she would not feel her stomach unclench until they were all safely across. The roar of the unseen water seemed to get louder.

"Busy hands, Willow," her mother said, as Mr. Hansen started back toward the front of the wagon train. Willow nodded, but there was little to do besides wait. She went and peeked into the back of the wagon. Anna was still sleeping heavily, her hair plastered to her forehead with sweat. Willow loosened the closure a little more.

It was hot. Willow brought the mules up closer to the wagon where they could get a little shade. She patted them and talked to them, fussing with their packs the way Jordan did. Jordan. Was he already in the muddy water?

Willow had watched her brother swim two other rivers, both much smaller than the flooded South Platte. She knew how it was done. The men would tie a rope around his waist and hold it, paying out the line as he swam. This was for Jordan's sake. If he lost his wind or hurt himself on rocks or debris, they could at least pull his body from the river if they couldn't save him. Jordan would carry a knife so that he could cut himself free if the rope washed into a snagged tree or rocks and got tangled. In his teeth, Jordan would have one end of a thin cord, so that when he climbed out on the far bank, even if he had somehow wriggled free of the rope around his waist or had to cut it, there would be a line across the river. If all went well, there would be two. But this river was so *wide*.

Willow gulped in a breath and saw her mother glance at her sharply.

"School in your thoughts, Miss Willow, or you will have us all in a panic."

Willow tried to obey, but it was impossible.

"Well, I am going to sit and rest a bit," Willow's

mother said. She went to the back of the wagon and leaned in, emerging with a cheese crate that she carried to the little band of shade beside the wagon. Turning it over, she sat down heavily, and Willow knew her thoughts were with Jordan as well. How could she think about anything else?

Once her brother made it across with both the cord and the rope, the men would tie thicker, stouter ropes to their ends, and Jordan would pull those across, fixing them to a solid anchor—a rock or a tree trunk. Once the ropes were strung, he would swim back, striking off upstream of the ropes, marked by lines of white where they chattered under the force of the muddy water, cutting into it as it passed.

Willow walked to the back of the wagon and peered in. Anna was still sleeping, her face wrinkled into a frown. How would it be for her in the ferry? Willow knew they were luckier than most of the people on the wagon train. Many of them couldn't swim a lick. She was nowhere near as good a swimmer as her older brothers, but she and Anna could both stroke pretty well. Willow had loved diving down into their little pond and watching the fish.

"Stop shaking and threatening to burst out crying every second," Willow ordered herself in a furious whisper. Fancy whimpered, hearing her and supposing she was angry with him.

"Fancy can ride with you in whatever wagon we ferry in, I imagine," her mother said, smiling reassuringly from where she sat in the shade of the wagon, close to the driver's bench. "In a few hours, we will be done with rivers for quite some time. Creeks perhaps, but nothing like this one."

Willow nodded, trying to calm herself. For once, when she most needed to occupy herself, there was nothing she could do.

Half an hour later, the wagons had all been moved closer to the fording place. "Break into groups of three wagons," Mr. Gaufer called out, standing on the back step of their wagon and shouting so that as many as possible could hear him. "Pick three that even each other out. Let's put big wagons with small, folks who are goods-heavy with those who have less. Folks with older children with folks who have little ones who need holding as we cross. Please be practical and fair in this. The first two groups, get unloaded and stacked—all three wagons' worth in one area."

A murmuring rose from the people around him, and he waited until it had died down. "Be patient and courteous, please. Pull out of line to group together, and move forward steadily as your turns come up.

When you get to the front, unload and unhitch all but your wheelers. We will organize to get goods down to the river's edge as we need them. Empty wagons will move past the ford and wait. I want as few wagons down close as possible until it's time to put them into the water. It's muddy enough."

People began to whisper to one another, discussing whom to include in their groups. Mr. Gaufer waited until the murmuring died down. "We'll swim the stock last. Make sure every family has enough cowherds left on this side to help with that. Everybody will have to work hard if we are to make it across before dark. Understand?"

There were murmurs of assent and one or two questions. Then Mr. Gaufer left, walking fast, climbing onto a wagon step farther down the line, and shouting out his instructions again.

"There's Jordan!" Willow saw her mother's face light up. Her voice sounded like a hallelujah in church.

Willow whirled around and felt a weight lift from her heart. Jordan's hair was plastered to his skull, and he had put his trousers and shirt back on over his wet underwear. There were big wet spots where his saturated longhandles were soaking through. His face was flushed high over each cheekbone, but his lips were pale and bluish.

"Get it across all right?" Mr. Hansen called.

Jordan nodded, wiping at his nose. "Yes, sir. It's wide and pretty rough. We pulled three lines across. They are going to use a guide rope."

"That should work fine," Mr. Hansen said briskly, glancing once at Willow's mother. Willow saw Jordan's expression change when he caught the hint.

"Yes, sir. Mr. Gaufer measured extended lines and figured the river width to a hair." He raised his hands in a gesture of admiration. "The lengths of rope were perfect, first try."

Mr. Hansen nodded. "He is a fine captain. We are lucky to have him."

"Yes, sir." Jordan stood uncertainly for a moment.

"You ought to change into dry clothes," Willow's mother said, but Jordan shook his head.

"It's hot, Mama. I'll dry soon enough and be cooler 'til then, is all."

Mr. Hansen cleared his throat. "We'll go with John Campbell, I think, and Eric Banner. He's a steady man, and it's a small wagon. And they need help with the little ones. I'll talk to them."

"And I'll check the mules," Jordan said.

As they walked away, Willow saw her mother turn and look at the wagon. After a moment or two she squared her shoulders and faced Willow again. "I suppose the first thing for us is to get Anna comfortable somewhere out of harm's way."

Willow turned a slow circle, taking in the earth, strewn with hail-beaten grass. It wasn't exactly muddy, but it was wet. And the sun was blazing down on them, hot on her shoulders and face.

"Under the wagon?" she suggested tentatively.

Willow watched her mother frown, thinking. "Maybe." She lifted her head to call to Jordan. "Run and ask your stepfather if we are going to have to move farther up or if we can unhitch here." Jordan nodded and started off. Willow and her mother watched him for a few seconds, then looked at each other.

"By tonight, Willow, it'll be done."

Willow tried to smile, feeling fear touch the back of her neck. It wouldn't be long before she had to climb into a wagon bed with empty water barrels lashed beneath it. She would have to watch the rush of murderous brown water slide beneath her feet.

CHAPTER EIGHT

They moved the wagon out of line, Mr. Hansen driving a little way off onto the prairie where they had enough room to work, then forward until they were within sight of the crossing place. Mr. Hansen turned the team in a wide arc, then pulled them to a stop.

Jordan pointed out the curve that made the river slow a little and the wide, easy slant of the land down to the water's edge. But it looked much the same as the rest of the river to Willow. There were cottonwood trees along the far side. Some were standing so deep in water that their trunks were invisible. They looked like giant, improbable bushes with their huge branches snaking out of the muddy water.

There were groups of three forming up all along the road. Some of the drivers saw what Mr. Hansen had done and imitated his wide turn so that their wagons ended up facing the crossing, too.

The Banners and the Campbells drove their teams up carefully, easing along, one on either side, then coming to a stop, the Banners in front by a dozen feet, the Campbells back about twenty, making a ragged little line of three. As people alighted there was a great deal of pointing and calling out of instructions. Then the voices fell and they all set to work.

Mr. Hansen and Jordan built a little lean-to for shade out of a sheet and four stout willow sticks from down by the river. Then they carried Anna out of the wagon, plank bed and all. She looked worse, somehow, in the sunlight. Her face seemed beyond pale; it was bloodless. Even her lips were lighter than they should have been. But when Mr. Hansen and Jordan positioned her beneath the temporary little shade they had made, she propped herself up to watch the work.

Willow let Fancy go to Anna, but she stayed close, ready to pluck him up if he got too rambunctious. At first he was obnoxious, licking Anna's face and pawing playfully at her hands. But after a moment or two he seemed to understand that she could only lie quietly, and he curled up beside her, enjoying her affection as he followed the progress of the unloading with his bright brown eyes.

Willow kept glancing over at Anna as she started unloading the wagon. For quite a while Anna met her eyes almost every time and smiled. But then she began to drowse again, lying back, one arm flung over her eyes to keep the fierce sunlight at bay. The sheet stretched over the pole frame above Anna's head fluttered in an increasing breeze as Willow, Jordan, and their mother emptied the wagon.

Bored with lying still beside Anna, Fancy trotted back and forth as the work went on, excited by so many people crisscrossing between the wagons, the loud voices and quick steps. Jordan carried load after load of the heavy flour and sugar sacks, laying the cotton bags carefully onto the painted canvas ground cloths Willow's mother had spread out. Willow and her mother carried lighter goods, including their stores of herbs and medicines, the dried vegetables in their thick canvas bags, and the heavy brown bags of salt. Willow's mother carried the small sack of coffee beans very carefully.

Lately they had been drinking raspberry tea. Her mother hated it, but she drank it every morning because Mr. Hansen insisted. Willow didn't mind the taste of it. In fact, she kind of liked it.

They had stopped to pick berries along a creek in Missouri and had run into two neighbor women who had come to pick as well. One of them had been elderly and had seemed to know a great deal about roots and herbs and what would heal what. She had said that raspberry leaf tea was good for women, especially those carrying a child, and that had convinced Mr. Hansen to let them stay an extra hour to pick and clean the leaves—once their berry baskets were full, of course.

"That's it for the stores," Jordan said, sliding the last of the bean sacks to the ground. Willow looked at their provisions. They had flour, beans, peas, dried vegetables, and a little smoked venison. Lying out here on the open ground, their pile of provisions seemed small to her, and she wondered if they could possibly make it to California on so little food.

"Willow?"

Her mother was standing beside the wagon. "Help Jordan with the trunk." Willow nodded and went into the wagon first. Jordan always walked backward when they carried things because he knew that she hated it.

As they set the trunk down, Willow's mother smiled. "We needed to do this anyway." She said it with the kind of fierce cheerfulness that Willow had come to realize was a cover for her fear and worry.

"We did," Willow agreed, admiring her mother and trying to imitate her. "Perhaps we will have a dry day tomorrow."

Her mother nodded approvingly. "That would be wonderful—give us a chance to dry everything thoroughly after the crossing." She began to restack the tin washbasins, fitting them more tightly together.

Willow went back to the wagon and wrapped her diary inside a cotton skirt and pushed it into a little bag that held the rest of her clothing, tying it tightly shut with a piece of cord. When she came out, she opened the trunk and put her bag inside.

She had already worn out one blouse and hopelessly stained all her clothes with berry juice and dirt and cooking grease and fire soot. By the time they got to California, she wasn't going to have a single stitch worth putting on.

If they got to California. Willow tried to work a little harder to shake such gloomy thoughts from her mind, but the sound of the river hissing against its banks was louder here.

Mr. Campbell and his sons carried their goods. They stacked their things in an orderly fashion on

India rubber ground cloths, all carefully placed so that nothing was damaged, or would be later, by moisture seeping into it from the ground.

Mr. Banner worked alone. None of his children was old enough to help and his wife was preoccupied with watching them to make sure they didn't get hurt wandering through the crowds of hurried adults, who walked with arms full or led mules or horses or oxen back toward the main herd.

While Willow and Jordan unloaded the wagon, Mr. Hansen unharnessed all but the wheeler yoke of oxen and led them, their great horns lowered in the wearying heat, toward the rear of the wagon train. The two wheelers would be enough to move the empty wagon down to the water's edge when the time came.

Jordan nearly stumbled over Fancy once, his arms full of their folded tents, but he was too busy to be angry for more than an instant. Willow whistled, and Fancy ran to join her.

"Do what you can with these," Willow's mother instructed, handing her a beeswax candle and a little box of bottles. One of them held their lucifer matches, several others were stoppered bottles of medicine, and one was the bottle of ink she used when she wrote in her diary. Willow lit the wick, then tipped the candle sideways, dripping wax over the top of the little stoppered bottle of laudanum, then the ink. The other seals still looked sound. Last, she carefully sealed the matches jar, dripping the wax around the rim until it was a solid, firm coating over the rim of the flat zinc lid.

Willow watched the people around her, stealing glances as she went about her own work. It had amazed her, the first time they had had to unload the wagons, how differently people packed. What people chose to leave behind and what they chose to take said a lot about them. How they took care of what they had brought told even more. Willow smiled, looking at the Campbells' bricklayer-straight piles standing next to the Banners' tumble of goods. Willow was equally fond of both families.

Once the wagon was empty, Jordan asked Mr. Hansen if he should go help the Banners. "That would be good, Jordan," Mr. Hansen answered. "We want everyone ready at about the same time, and the sooner the better. Mr. Gaufer told me they will take those first who are ready first." He glanced upward, toward the west, where the cloud bank still boiled and threatened. "It would be good to get across as soon as we can."

The storm clouds hadn't moved much in the last two hours, but that didn't mean they wouldn't. They had seen a lot of storms rise so suddenly there was no time to do more than circle the wagons.

"Levin will stay with the stock?" Jordan asked, turning toward the Banner wagon.

Mr. Hansen smiled one of his tight little smiles. "For now, yes. But you and I will help when it comes time to swim them over. I want to start ours in upstream this time—maybe farther than the others will."

"Willow?" Anna's voice was breathless.

Willow looked over to see Fancy dancing around Anna, obviously delighted to find her awake again. Willow whistled and Fancy bounded toward her, gathering himself to leap as he got close. Willow caught him and swung around, setting him back down immediately. She heard a little gasp of appreciation and turned to see the Banner brood staring at her. In the center of the children stood Mrs. Banner. She smiled and came close, somehow walking in the center of all her children, like a goose swimming across a grassy pond with her goslings circling, fussing, peeking through her feathers.

"He is an adorable little dog, Willow," Mrs. Banner said kindly, reaching to pat Fancy's head. Two of her children began to quibble, standing toe to toe. Mrs. Banner picked the younger one up, setting him on her hip. The difference in elevations seemed enough to end the argument. Fancy trotted to the closest of the Banner children, a boy of about eight and a girl about four. They began to giggle and pat him.

"Thank you, ma'am," Willow said. "He is good; just sometimes he gets a little rambunctious."

"Willow, don't stop working." This was Mr. Hansen's voice, stern and flat. "I apologize for her keeping you from your own concerns, Mrs. Banner."

Mrs. Banner smiled and shook her head. She might have been able to tell Mr. Hansen that she had been the one to start the conversation if she had been quicker. As it was, he had turned his back to them as he untied the string of mules. He had already unloaded them all, had stacked the goods they had carried, then made a pile of their packsaddles.

Willow watched him, angry. She almost never dallied. She did everything she was told and a good deal more. Did he have to embarrass her in front of Mrs. Banner by talking to her as if she were a little child?

Mr. Hansen was whistling, moving briskly. Once he had the halter rope freed, he walked the lead animal in a wide circle. The others, tied muzzle-to-tail, followed. Mr. Hansen straightened out the lead mule and led the animals toward the rear of the train, where he would leave them with Levin and the other cowherds. Willow, caught staring, tried to step aside and bumped into Mrs. Banner, who pulled her children to one side.

"Get the cover off the wagon, Willow," Mr. Hansen said without looking at her. He passed, and the mules shuffled after him, their heads down and their tails low. They were more than tired, Willow realized. They were listless from hunger.

Willow turned back to work. She could hear high, sharp shouts from the rear of the wagon train as the cowherds worked to keep all the stock under control. Among all the families, there were three hundred head of stock. It was quite a job.

"Listen to them," Willow's mother called. "They sound like a bunch of cowboys whooping like that." She smiled tightly. "Karl says Levin is good at herding."

Willow nodded. She didn't like herding. She was always afraid it would be her sudden move—or Fancy's—that would send the animals running the wrong way, scattered like flung sand across the prairie. Even if no one got hurt, it took days to gather up the stock, and they had twice lost a few animals to injury or Indians after stampedes.

Her family had eight oxen, six mules, and four

cows, one of them a freshened milker. So far, they had lost none. Willow hated the stampedes. Once they began to run, the animals were like a torrent of hooves and flesh that pounded along with no more mindfulness than a river. She had heard many stories of children being killed in stampedes. Mercifully, it had not happened to anyone on their train.

"Willow, start the cover," her mother directed. "I'll help in a minute."

Willow began untying the wagon cover. She had untied all the cords and was rolling up the cover, starting at the back, when her mother came to help. Together they wrestled the heavy canvas from the arched wooden bows that held it above the wagon bed.

"Willow?" Anna called again.

Willow started toward her. Fancy bounded over to Anna, licking her face. Anna laughed, but it was a strained sound. Willow caught Fancy up in her arms.

"Willow, would you mind bringing me water again?"

Willow shook her head. "Of course not, Anna. Do you want something to eat? There's hard bread. Or an apple?"

Anna shook her head, making a face. "The idea

of eating makes me feel sick. It was so hot in that wagon, Willow—"

"I know," Willow said, looking closely at her sister. A little color had come back into her face. Maybe the heat in the wagon was making her sicker than a draft would. It wasn't good for her not to eat—she would just get weaker.

Willow looked up. Jordan and her mother were helping Mr. Banner now. So was Mrs. Campbell. That meant they were getting close.

Fancy at her heels, Willow hurried. She found a crust of hard bread and an apple, then ran to fill the cup. She laid everything on the edge of Anna's cot, brushing at the little balls of prairie soil that Fancy had tracked onto the bedding.

"The apple smells good, Willow," Anna said. "Maybe I am a little hungry." She smiled, and for a second she almost looked like her usual, merry self.

Willow smiled back at Anna, glad to see a spark in her sister's eyes. As she stood up, she noticed the sound of the river again and realized she had been ignoring it. She turned to look. The water was brown and wide. So wide.

CHAPTER NINE

The men picked four wagons that had tightly fitted planks. All four were made from seasoned white oak—it didn't shrink in the dry weather, causing cracks to appear between the planks.

Mr. Gaufer presided over the work, directing the men this way and that. Using one pair of wheeler oxen, each of the four wagons was pulled out of line and backed slowly down into the water. Then, a half-dozen men turned the wagons over while another group gathered the tightest water barrels to be found on the train.

Using pitch to recaulk any seam that looked

even slightly unsound, and looping the ropes through the wheel spokes, they tied the barrels to the underside of the wagons.

As they worked, the men talked and sometimes argued over the best way to do things. Mr. Gaufer walked back and forth, calming one man, encouraging another. All of them kept glancing at the sky. The line of dark clouds in the west had expanded and thickened, but if it was moving toward them, it was moving slowly. Willow watched Mr. Gaufer as he directed the men; anything was better than staring at the brown water and listening to the sound of her own heart.

"Repack the dried vegetables, Willow. I would imagine we can fit them into one box instead of two now."

Willow turned, startled out of her thoughts. Her mother was smiling, but her eyes were intense. "School in your feelings, Willow. Anna is frightened enough without you mooning around like this. Stop staring. Busy hands."

Willow nodded and set to work repacking. Fancy circled her, whining a little, seemingly aware of her uneasiness. Willow picked him up for a second, burying her face in his warm fur. Then she set to work. She condensed the dried vegetables into one box and helped her mother shake out the linens and refold them in the trunk. Fancy fussed and worried about her feet.

"Stop that, Fancy," Willow's mother scolded him. "We don't need anything else dampening our moods." Fancy paced a little ways away, then lay down, looking at Willow with anxious eyes. Willow took a deep breath, and her mother caught her eye.

"We can use this time to go through the apples."

Together they sorted through the big baskets of apples they had bought in the last farming community they had passed through almost a month before. Close to the bottom, Willow found one that had been bruised and was rotting. She pulled it out and held it close to her nose to breathe in the sweet, winey scent.

"That one would have ruined them all within a week or two," her mother said approvingly.

"We're getting close down here," Mr. Gaufer called out. Willow jerked around, all her practiced calmness evaporating.

Willow had not allowed herself to watch the men for a while; since she had last looked, they had pulled side boards from other wagons and raised the sides of the four they would use as ferries. Now they had four ferries with planked railings about three feet high. Mr. Gaufer was walking up the bank.

"You first," he called to the Cleats, a big family with several married sisters and their husbands and children traveling together. Their three wagons were closest to the crossing.

"Then Banners, Campbells, and Hansens." He pointed at Willow—or at least it felt like he had pointed directly at her. Her heart beat harder. Willow took a deep breath.

"Gastons and Daniels go third," Mr. Gaufer called out as he walked past. His voice faded as he got farther down the line. People he had already passed began talking to one another. Willow heard the shrill voice of Mrs. Snyder, and she hoped that the argument over the piano wouldn't get out of hand. Sometimes, she found herself blushing at the Snyders' battles. How could they yell at each other like that in front of so many other people?

"Set off, set off!"

Willow turned toward the river again. There were six men standing in one of the ferry wagons. They had fastened a loop of rope over one of the lines that Jordan had tied off on the far side. It would slide along, like a moveable anchor, to help keep them from drifting downstream under the fierce pressure of the current. But since there wasn't anyone on the far bank to pull them across yet, they would have to do it themselves.

Shouting and gesturing, the men brought the towrope into the wagon and began to haul themselves across, working together, hand over hand. Willow watched them. They barely seemed to move. It took a long time before they got to the center of the river, and they seemed to slow even more. Finally, they were on the opposite bank. They looked small and helpless as they jumped over the side and waded out. One of them lagged behind, bending to check the towrope that had been tied to the buckboard seat. He straightened and waved his hands above his head, signaling.

"Let's have some hands here," Mr. Gaufer yelled as he came back up the line. "Let's get the Cleats' belongings down to the water's edge now. And move their wagons on past. Let's get some help here!"

"Willow?" Her mother motioned for her to respond to the call. "You go. I'll stay up here with Anna and Fancy. Fancy? Come here." Fancy looked mournfully at Willow.

"Stay with Mama, Fancy. Stay here." He whined but obeyed. As she walked away, Willow heard Anna calling Fancy and smiled but didn't look back. Sometimes, if she turned around, Fancy thought it was all right to come with her. And it wasn't. With this many people walking back and forth, he would only get underfoot.

Willow and everyone who was within earshot and not working at something else pitched in carrying the Cleats' belongings. Men, women, and children walked in a ragged line, their arms filled with boxes, sacks, and stacks of the Cleats' goods.

As she walked downhill, Willow watched the men on her side of the river. Seven or eight of them lined up along the towrope and began to pull the wagon back across the water. With men on both banks they could now pull full wagons across and empty ones back.

Willow glanced at the sky to the west as she walked back up the bank. The clouds were still, piling higher and getting a little darker. She saw a wink of lightning, but maybe it was going to be a dry storm.

The Cleats' worldly belongings were slowly transferred to the ferry wagons. It would take two trips of the ferry to carry across what one wagon could hold—the stacks had to be both lower and more stable because the coverless wagon would heave and lean in the rough water.

We are like giant ants, Willow thought, as she gathered up an ax, a hatchet, and two shovels. She started down the bank again, passing empty-handed people on their way up. Willow had to smile in spite of her nervousness. Like ants at a huge picnic.

As people from the back of the wagon train came forward to watch, the Cleats' first load of goods made it across. It was obvious the wagon was harder to hold against the current once it was weighted down with a full load. Willow could hear the men grunting with the effort.

While Willow and the others loaded the second ferry wagon, the men on the far bank made quick work of unloading the first. Willow had gone up and down the bank only three more times, carrying loads as big as she could manage, when she heard the murmur along the bank that made her stop and look. The men on the far bank were waving; this was the signal to bring back the unloaded wagon.

Immediately, the men on the towrope set to work, pulling the wagon back across. This time it seemed harder. The men fighting the rope were silent and grim, grunting and sweating fiercely in the hot sun.

As the empty wagon got closer, Willow noticed something odd—a roil of white water on the downstream side. As the men heaved together, shouting to time their efforts, the wagon wallowed into the shallows, and Willow saw a thick cottonwood branch, its leaves swaying in the water. It was caught in the struts of the wagon tongue. As the men drew the wagon close, one of them waded out to free the branch. He dragged at it, his arms wrapped around the rough bark, then straightened. He cupped his hands around his mouth and faced the watchers. "Someone got a saw handy? This is wedged tight."

"I do," Mr. Banner called, and he scrambled up the bank to get it.

"It must be flooding upstream," Mrs. Holliday called out. "Look, there's more."

Murmurs ran through the watchers as they stared at the muddy water rushing past. Willow saw a rill of white water moving along with the current and realized it was another branch. She glanced at the dark line of clouds. They still hadn't advanced, but she could just make out sheets of blurred gray beneath them. It was raining west of them now. Would it make the river rise even higher?

Mr. Banner came back down the bank carrying a long saw with a handle on either end. He waded into the water and placed the long notched blade across the branch. The first man hesitated, then said something that Willow couldn't hear and repositioned the saw.

"Look at *that*!"

Willow recognized Mr. Hansen's voice. She turned to see him pointing out over the water.

Everyone raised their eyes to see what he was talking about. At first, Willow saw nothing. Then she noticed a long patch of foamy water near the center of the wide channel.

"That's big," one of the Banner children said behind her.

"It is," Mr. Banner agreed.

"As you can all see," Mr. Gaufer called out, "there is debris in the water. It looks like mostly logs and big branches washed out from some flooded place upstream."

"Do you think it's safe to cross now?" Willow turned to see Mr. Hansen standing solidly, his hands on his hips.

Mr. Gaufer nodded. "I do. There is always a chance that—"

His words were cut short by a high, whining sound. Willow jerked back around. It took her a few seconds to understand what had happened. The floating branch had hit the guide rope. It was singing with the impact, rising up out of the water as the tension stretched it taut. It shone wet in the sun, a long V shape spanning the river. Then the branch tumbled in the water, clearing the rope. It relaxed, sagging back into position.

"Come sit with Anna, Willow," her mother called, startling her. Willow turned to see her standing halfway down the slope. Willow nodded and walked toward her, making her way through the crowd.

"As soon as Jordan is finished, he and Karl are going to carry Anna down to the riverside," Willow's mother said as they walked up the hill together. "I want you to talk to her, stay with her a while."

Anna was sitting up again, and she looked upset. "I want to walk, Willow." Her normally sunny voice was full of tears. "I am so sick of everyone having to do everything for me." She rocked back and forth, working her weight onto her elbows so she could raise her body off the cot, but she didn't try to stand up. Her face was no longer pale. She was flushed.

"It's steep, Anna. And muddy. It's better if they carry you," Willow said, squatting down.

"My foot hurts so bad, Willow," Anna said. "Is the river really wide? I can hear it."

Willow hesitated, considered fibbing, then discarded the idea. Anna would see it for herself soon enough. "Except for the Missouri, it's the widest we've crossed yet," Willow answered truthfully. "By far. And it's brown and muddy."

Anna lay back down, keeping her eyes on Willow's. "You remember the day Papa drowned?"

Willow nodded. "Every second of it."

Anna closed her eyes. "So do I."

Fancy pushed his muzzle into Willow's side, nudging her hard enough to push her sideways. She recovered her balance and glanced back to find Anna's eyes open.

"I hope California is worth all this," Anna said very quietly.

Willow nodded. "I do, too."

Anna nodded and exhaled. "Everyone says it only gets harder from here on."

Willow nodded. It scared her. How would they manage if the trail got worse? Just then, Willow saw people beginning to come up the hill to help carry their belongings down to the ferries. She saw Mr. Campbell and Mr. Banner pick up their trunk, and she thought about her diary tucked deep inside. By tonight she would be able to write that they were across the South Platte river.

"Willow?" She looked up to see Mr. Hansen and Jordan walking toward her. "It's time to carry Anna down."

Willow squeezed Anna's hand and stood up. Anna wiped her eyes. "We're just about ready down here," Mr. Gaufer yelled. Mr. Hansen and Jordan lifted Anna's cot and walked slowly toward the river. Willow followed them.

At the river's edge, Willow stood stiffly

by Anna's cot, holding Fancy, watching. The Campbells were nearby, and just behind them, the Banners. The men and older boys helped load, then pitched in with the rope hauling.

Willow could feel Anna looking up at her, and she fought to keep a false smile on her face. The ferries carrying all their goods made it across the river. One splintered cottonwood branch came down the river while the wagons were being pulled across, but it floated over the guide rope without a problem.

"Willow?"

She whirled around, startled, even though she had been expecting Mr. Hansen's voice, had been waiting for it. He was holding her mother's hand. Jordan was already walking toward Anna's cot. It was time to go. Trembling, Willow turned to face the river.

CHAPTER TEN

Mr. Hansen was not going with them, nor Mr. Banner, nor Mr. Campbell. All the men and boys were staying to help ferry the wagons across, then swim the stock.

The ferry wagon was pulled close to the bank so that only a narrow strip of about three feet of water and mud had to be stepped across. Anna was carried on first. Her plank cot was laid across the wagon, all the way at the front. Anna struggled to sit up, leaning against the side boards. Jordan jumped back across the mud to stand on the bank.

"Come on, Willow," Mr. Hansen said from the open gate of the ferry. Still holding Fancy, she stood at the very edge of the shallow water, hesitating. Mr. Hansen reached for her free hand. Jordan boosted her from behind as Mr. Hansen pulled her forward. Together they lifted her over the water and set her on the wagon planks. She stood uncertainly for a second, startled by the rocking sway of the ferry on the water.

Willow's mother embraced Mr. Hansen and said something in a low voice. He nodded and patted her hand, then lifted her up and across the water. Willow tucked Fancy close under one arm and extended her free hand to steady her mother. Then, together, they went to stand beside Anna at the front of the wagon. Willow turned and faced the shoreline, looking for Jordan, trying to ignore the steady drumming of her own pulse. Soon they would be across. Soon this would be over.

Mr. Banner lifted his children into the wagon bed one at a time. Willow smiled when they laughed in delight at seeing Fancy, but her heart was not in the smile.

Mrs. Banner was helped in and she gathered her children close. They stood in their usual semi-circle around her, each with one small hand on her skirts, the other picking a nose or twisting a lock of hair. They were pretty children, Willow heard herself think. She counted them, something she had never done before because they were usually too much in motion. There were five, and the eldest couldn't be more than eight.

The Campbell women got on. Ariel and Alexandra climbed up without help, getting the hems of their skirts and their shoes wet and muddy. They both turned to help their mother, not that she seemed to need it. They stood solidly at the end gate of the ferry.

"All ready?" Mr. Gaufer asked.

The Banner children set up a shout, and the Campbell women nodded politely in their quiet, cheerful way. Willow glanced at her mother. Her eyes were hard and bright as she nodded, her mouth set in a thin line. Mr. Gaufer closed the wagon gate, then stepped back and to one side. He raised both arms over his head, signaling the men on the towline on the far side.

The wagon bed rocked beneath Willow's feet, and everyone had to grab a side board as it dipped to one side, then the other under the sudden pressure on the rope. Willow gripped the side board with one hand, holding Fancy tightly against her side with the other. The wagon creaked and shivered as it began to move, and Anna made a little sound of fear. Willow cried out softly without meaning to.

Her mother looked at her, hard. "Don't scare your sister." Willow swallowed and nodded, as her mother squatted down to talk to Anna.

When they left the calmer water of the shallows and were pulled toward the central channel of the river, the ferry rolled beneath Willow's feet. She could see the men on the far bank bent double, hauling on the towrope that dragged the ferry wagon relentlessly into the wide brown river. Fancy wriggled and whined a little. Two of the Banner children were crying; the others were wide-eyed and still. The Campbell girls and their mother each picked a child to hold, and Mrs. Banner, left with only the two who wept, comforted and crooned.

"It's not as bad as being in the wagon all closed up," Willow heard Anna say. "At least I can see the sky." Willow looked down at her sister and smiled. Fancy was looking out across the water, his eyes bright and alert.

Suddenly the ferry hit a crest of water head on and bucked, dipping low in front, then rising again. Anna gasped and grabbed at Willow's leg for support. Fancy yelped as Willow clutched him tighter, trying to regain her own balance. Had they hit a sandbar?

"Hold on," Willow's mother commanded her.

Willow braced herself against the sideboards, leaning hard. Fancy squirmed, but she managed to hold onto him. She pulled in a deep breath, looking upstream over the muddy water surrounding them. Here and there it was capped with white foam. She stared, squinting into the bright sun. Her legs felt weak.

"Oh, dear Lord," Willow heard her mother breathe, and she shivered, knowing that what she had feared was true. The roaring river was suddenly full of floating tree limbs and splintered trunks. Some flooded place upstream was giving up whole trees to the force of the water.

"Here's another. Hang on!" This was Mrs. Campbell's voice. This time the limb hit them side-long and scraped heavily along the side of the ferry, a terrible, screaming sound as the branch ground against it. The ferry bobbed and shuddered again, but the guide rope held them steady on their course, and the limb washed past, turning slowly in the water as it hit the guide rope. For a second the rope held it back, then it floated free.

Fancy whimpered low in his throat, and Willow realized how tightly she had been holding him. She released the pressure and lifted him close. He licked her cheek. Willow felt Anna's hand on her leg and looked down.

Anna was as white as snowfall, her eyes darting from one side of the ferry to the other. Willow's mother, almost as pale as Anna, was gripping the side board. Her lips were moving slightly, and Willow knew she was praying for their safety. There were shouts from the far bank, and Willow saw the men bent nearly double, hauling on the towline as hard as they could. She looked back toward the wagon and saw a boy standing off to one side, his arms crossed. Jordan was still watching. She looked for Mr. Hansen but the bank was too far away now—the crowd blended together, a wash of faces.

Soon, Willow forced herself to think. Soon we will be across, and they will wait until the trees have gone past before they continue ferrying.

An explosive shudder wracked the ferry, and Willow almost fell. Anna screamed, and their mother dropped to her knees beside her. Willow whirled, facing upstream. A massive tree trunk had hit them, sliding back along the current from the impact. Its roots spreading like clawing fingers, so big that it rose from the water higher than their heads, the tree came forward, shoved by the muddy water. It slammed into the ferry a second time, and their screams and squeals were lost in the snapping and grinding of wood on wood.

The ferry rocked and swayed, and then, suddenly, it felt loose and odd beneath Willow's feet. A second later she saw an odd tannish squiggle arcing back over the water and realized that the guide rope had snapped. The massive weight of the tree pressing against the ferry had stretched it past its strength.

Fancy was frantic with fear. He twisted against Willow's chest just as the ferry was slammed again.

The enormous tangle of roots loomed over them once more, then it skidded off to one side, swirling in the current behind them.

Willow could only stare at the universe of dark water that roared and swirled around them. She knew that the towrope could break now, and that if it did, they would be careening down the river in a wooden box, helpless to guide the wagon or save themselves.

She closed her eyes and prayed, then opened them to see the men on the far bank working in unison. Fragments of a shouted chant were thrown out over the water, along with their cries of warning. The men seemed farther away, not closer, and the angle had changed. The ferry had drifted a long way down the river. Fancy wriggled again. He was panicked now, and she could not find a single calming word, not a single shred of her own courage. All she could do was hold him tightly and wait. After a moment, he stopped trying to escape her arms.

Willow lowered her eyes to avoid looking at the water. Anna and her mother cowered together, embracing, their eyes closed as they prayed. The Banner children were silent, clutching at the Campbell girls or their mother or one another. Mrs. Campbell had begun to pray aloud, asking for courage and strength. Fancy struggled a little more, then subsided.

The current shoved at the ferry, and it shivered

and ducked under the strain. Then they slid down a glassy curve in the current, and once more the enormous tree stump rose above them. Fancy hid his head against Willow's body. Anna screamed. Willow looked down into the murky water and saw the limbs, some angling straight down, others lying just beneath the surface, their leaves moving in perfect, helpless unison with the changes in the current. She was staring at them when the tree slammed into the ferry, straight on this time, a gigantic hammer blow that made the side planks heave inward, splintering.

Water rushed inward, and Willow tried to hold onto Fancy, tried to reach for her sister, but couldn't manage to do either. Anna was screaming. Fancy fell sideways, hitting hard, then scrambled to his feet. The ferry wallowed sideward, the towrope rising off the surface of the river with the tension. The tree rolled in the water, and an enormous limb was suddenly beside Willow, seeming to reach through the bowed planks, its twigs hooking her skirt, tangling leaves in her hair, pulling her forward.

Before she could react or even think, Willow was in the water, feeling the impossible coldness seep into her clothing, her skin. She cried out and saw Fancy leap up, over the planks, a high, arcing jump that landed him in the river beside her. Then the tree turned, dragging her beneath the water.

CHAPTER ELEVEN

Willow fought with the tree, tearing her hair loose from its clutching grasp, then her dress, then kicking hard, pulling herself through the water, aiming for the muted sunlight she could see through the drowning cottonwood leaves.

As she burst from the surface of the water, Willow dragged in one long, ragged breath after another, choking. The river surged and shimmered all around her, rushing her along. She could hear her mother's voice calling, screaming, but could not see her, could only fight to breathe.

Once she stopped choking, Willow thrashed at

the water, turning to look upstream. She couldn't see the ferry. Or Fancy. Her thoughts were stricken to silence, and terror gripped her heart. Willow turned in the water again, a full circle, unbelieving. Had they been that close to a bend in the river? Willow couldn't remember.

Willow scanned the width of the brown river, gulping in a mouthful of water when the shape of the current carried her higher, then let her fall. She couldn't see anything except the empty banks and endless muddy water. Willow's heart sank a little, her spirit ebbing. Then, suddenly, she felt a tug at her skirt and splashed, slapping at the water to turn herself, terrified that the tree had risen beneath her and was going to drag her down again.

Heart pounding, Willow waited, breathing hard from exertion and fear. She gulped water again and coughed, every inch of her skin expecting another touch, a deadly pull from beneath the water. It did not come. The moments passed.

Willow twisted hard, turning to look upstream again, searching frantically for some sign of the ferry. In the second before the tree had dragged her down, she had seen Fancy leap toward her. Where was he? Had the tree pulled him under, too? Willow shook off the unbearable thought, trying to focus upstream, squinting, praying for a glimpse of the ferry wagon. Of anything but brown water.

Willow's muscles were starting to ache and balk, the cold from the river seeping into her skin, her heart. She knew she should try to swim toward the bank, but she was afraid to put her face in the muddy water, to stop looking for the wagon ferry and Fancy—she was afraid of the darkness behind her closed eyes.

Willow flailed at the water, keeping her head up, kicking as hard as she could. She longed to take off her shoes, to free herself from her skirts. But it would be dangerous to try. What if she got tangled in her own skirts, or another limb came close while she was beneath the water, fiddling with her shoe buckles?

The current lifted her again, then shoved her to one side, around a gray rock jutting skyward. Willow tried to swim toward the shore. The water shoved her along roughly, pushing her around one long, curving bend, then another, sharper one. When she paused to tread water, trying to catch her breath, she was pretty sure she was even farther from the bank than she had been to start with.

As the river narrowed and dropped, roaring through a ravine, Willow barely managed to keep her head above water. She went under twice, the cold water closing over her head, but both times she fought her way up again. Then her left hand cramped, and she was afraid for a second that she would sink. She worked her hand into a fist, then forced it open against the knifelike pain. Clenching and unclenching her hand, Willow worked the cramp out and began to paddle again.

The ravine opened up, and the water around her slowed. Willow gasped for air, trying again to move across the current toward the far bank. She made some progress, then lost what she had gained when the river channel narrowed again, the current snaking sideways for a stretch, pulling her back out into the center.

Her face beaded with muddy water, teeth jibbering, Willow saw a big limb coming toward her. She dove face first into the water and redoubled her efforts to swim, but it was impossible to wrestle the massive current and win. Willow raised her head to look, trying frantically to get out of the way, but the limb, as big around as a water barrel, was suddenly so close that she could only turn to face it, pushing against it with her hands as it overtook her. The rough bark scraped her palms, then her shoulder and cheek, bruising her painfully.

For a few seconds, Willow was sure she would go back under the water. Then the log swung around in the water and was suddenly floating beside her, not running her down. Willow drew in a shuddering breath.

The log had a bend like an elbow about halfway along its length. Willow held on, eyes closed, her hands clawlike across the bark, grateful just to rest, to breathe without fighting to swim.

When her breath was slower and she could think, Willow worked her way along the log and found that where it bent, she could get her arm over it. The branch turned a little in the water and Willow cried out and thrashed with fear, but it went no farther.

Carefully, teeth still chattering with cold, Willow hauled herself out of the water and collapsed against the rough bark, elbows hooked over the top of the log. After a few minutes, she worked one leg up and straddled the log. She lay forward, joyful to be out of the muddy water, to be able to breathe without it finding its way into her mouth. Her mind seemed to quiet, and for a long time she simply lay there, breathing deeply, exhausted.

After a while Willow could feel the sun, still hot, beating on her skin. She wanted to raise her head but could not. She squeezed her eyes tighter and cried in relief and fear. When Willow finally opened her eyes and raised her head, she very nearly started crying again.

She had been too exhausted and too frightened to fight the river anymore, and the log had saved her life. It had also played the cruelest trick of all. It had drifted out of the swift current and into calmer, shallow water nearer the river bank—on the wrong side.

Willow wrenched around to stare at the far bank. It seemed too distant even to contemplate reaching, forever on the other side of the raging torrent that poured down the main channel of the river. She was nearing a bend, and the log spun slowly, eddying into even quieter water.

Trying not to cry, Willow leaned forward and began using her outspread palms for oars. It was easy to guide the log here, where the water was slow and shallow. After a few minutes of paddling, she could see the shape of rocks on the river bottom.

Willow managed to slide off the log, scraping her ankle painfully as she dragged her foot across, hopping clumsily, half falling in the shallows. She staggered to the edge, then stood, swaying. It took her another few minutes to find the strength to climb out. Once she was on dry land she sank to the ground and began to weep.

When Willow managed to get to her feet, she stood shivering and looked up at the sky. The sun was way past noon—maybe four o'clock. That meant she had been in the water about two hours, most of it probably lying on the log, floating fast.

Willow dragged in a shuddering breath. Her family would be sure she had drowned. What else could they think? Unless she could get back to the wagons before they were all across, she would be stranded. They would look for her a little, but they would not wait once all the wagons were across. They couldn't. They couldn't risk another day without grass for the stock—especially not while they were afraid of being delayed further by rain.

Willow lifted her still dripping skirts, then let them fall. She wrung the cloth out as best she could, looking helplessly upstream. How far had she come? It had to be miles. And she was so incredibly tired. Her legs weighed down by desperation and despair, Willow started walking.

Once she had scrambled up the bank and stood upon the prairie again, Willow followed the road she and her family had traveled. The ruts from the wagon wheels were deep, the ground pocked with hoofprints from their cattle.

Willow walked as fast as she could, weary in the slanting afternoon sun. Her thoughts whirled like river water. What had happened to her mother and Anna and the others? And Fancy? Her eyes stung, and she tried to push the thoughts away, but could not. If the tow rope had broken, she told herself, the ferry would have been swept downstream—and she would have seen it, she was pretty sure. Willow held that thought close; it was at least a little comfort and helped her push away thoughts of Fancy. Her family was probably all right. Probably. She willed it to be so, then felt her eyes sting again. How could she know for sure? Maybe the ferry had capsized.

Fresh anguish made Willow bend nearly double as she began to cry again. She forced herself to straighten, forced herself to keep walking. School in your fear, she told herself. Stop crying. Walk. Think what to do.

But what *could* she do if no one remained at the crossing? Willow glanced behind herself. Maybe there would be another wagon train before too long. But Willow knew this was false hope. Even if she could survive long enough, most wagons didn't come this far south—their wagon train had been pushed by rain and lack of grazing. As soon as the river went down, wagons would cross the South Platte farther north again. Willow inhaled deeply and let it out, hearing the trembling unevenness in her breath. She forced herself to lift her feet faster. The slap of her wet skirts against her legs made a lonely rhythm, quickly lost in the roar of the river.

At first Willow managed a fairly good pace. She had been walking since they had left home, after all. She was tired, but the muscles in her legs were hard and practiced. And her fear pushed her along. She watched the road at her feet, refusing to look up at the endless horizons very often, trying hard to shut out the immensity of prairie and the enormous vacancy of the sky overhead.

When Willow heard Fancy's faint barking, she thought she had imagined it. But the sound didn't diminish or fade, it got louder. Willow turned and stared in the direction of the river and saw him trotting toward her. She fell to her knees and held out her arms, crying hard. Her tears stung the deep scratches the log had left on her cheek. Fancy snuggled close, shivering, his sodden fur cold against her skin. When she could, Willow stood again, holding Fancy. She began walking. Their only chance was to hurry.

After a time, Willow noticed the quick, warm panting of Fancy's breath on her right arm. She looked down at him. His eyes were brighter now, and he wriggled in her arms. She set him on the ground, and he followed at her heels, his head and tail low, his fur matted with river silt, but keeping up. Willow put all of her mind and her heart into walking as the sun lowered in the sky. She would not stop, would not allow herself to slow down. But she was so tired. *Too tired.*

It was dusky when Willow finally came to the last bend. She recognized it because there were odd tracks, crisscrossing where the wagons had pulled out in groups of three. Her heart rising to an ache in her throat, she topped the last rise and looked down at the fording place, then across the river where the towropes had been tied off. Fancy stood close against her leg and she could feel the beating of his heart and her own.

There was nothing here now. Nothing but the very last of the daylight on the wide muddy river. As the sun went down, the river faded into the roaring silence of the endless black sky above the prairie.

CHAPTER TWELVE

Willow awakened before dawn. It took a moment for her to realize where she was and why she and Fancy were huddled together in the lee of a cottonwood tree. Willow uncurled slowly, her muscles sore and incredibly stiff. The bruises on her face and shoulder hurt, and the palms of her hands felt raw. The still, gray sky was dotted with clouds this morning. Some of them had the thick, heavy look that the rain clouds had had the day before.

Willow felt her heart constrict. It was as though God were playing cruel tricks on her. It wasn't enough that she had to be lonely and hungry and scared for her life. He was going to make it rain so she'd be cold and wet, too. And the river would stay high for days, until there was no hope of her crossing and catching up to the wagons. Not that there was any real hope of it anyway.

Fancy shook and stretched and sniffed the morning air. He licked her face and hands, over-joyed, as he always was, to see her. Willow smiled a little.

Fancy trotted a little way from Willow as she shook out her damp skirts. Startled by her sudden motion, a rabbit exploded out of the brush a few feet from them. Fancy barked at it. A second one ran at his commotion, and he chased it, streaking across the hail-flattened grass.

"Fancy!"

Willow watched him in the dawn light, half hoping he would catch the rabbit. She was hungry. But she knew he probably wouldn't. She had no knife to clean or skin a rabbit anyway and no fire to cook it on. She shivered, blinking as the rabbit dis-appeared and Fancy skidded to a stop, barking excit-edly at the hole it had gone down.

"Fancy!" Willow called again. He ignored her. He probably couldn't hear her over the noise he was making. Willow began to walk after him, calling as she went. She was well out into the open—too far from the trees to run for shelter—when she saw the Indian. He was watching her. He sat astride a dark bay horse and was leading a buckskin.

Willow stumbled to a halt, uncertain what to do. How could she have been so stupid, so careless? The Indian's hair hung straight down his back, the blue-black color of a raven's wing. A deer haunch was tied across the buckskin's back along with square leather bags that bulged with whatever was inside them. There were triangle designs on the leather in dark red and white.

Willow's knees felt weak, and she was afraid that she would collapse where she stood. Fancy finally looked up from his rabbit hole. He tore back to Willow, placing himself between her and the silent Indian, his forelegs stiff and his bark furious and frightened. The matted hair on his back rose in an angry ridge.

The Indian looked at Willow and made a motion that took in the river, her damp, muddy clothes, and the empty prairie. "Wagons go?" he called.

Willow edged backward. What would he do with her now? People were captured, sometimes killed. She stooped to pick up Fancy, to quiet him. He squirmed for a moment, then stopped barking and only growled, facing the Indian from his perch in her arms. The Indian's face did not change when she met his eyes again. He sat very still as though he were a stone or one of the trees that dotted the riverbank. Then, very slowly, he dismounted and walked toward her, leading the horses.

When he was close enough that Willow could see the dark blue beads sewn in a triangular pattern on his belt and the feather tied into his hair, he stopped. One more step and he would be able to reach her.

Willow was shaking with fear, and she knew that he could see it. Very slowly, he took something from a fringed leather pouch that hung from his belt. It was a small blue quinine bottle. Willow recognized it instantly, then recognized him. This was the Indian who had spoken to her mother, whose son had been sick.

The Indian turned to face the river. He made a leaping motion with his hand. "Want go?"

Willow had to swallow before she could answer, and even then her voice was raw. "Yes." She said it again, a little louder. "Oh, God, yes."

The Indian put one hand out, motioning for her to follow. Willow hesitated, then stumbled after him as he led his horses closer to the river. She stood shaking, glancing back and forth between the

Indian and the torrent of brown water. Fancy, quiet now, wanted down, but Willow held him tightly.

The Indian gestured and said something in his own language. Willow shook her head, not understanding. He reached out and touched the bruise on her cheek. Fancy growled, but the Indian ignored him. Turning quickly, he untied the leather thongs that held the deer meat on the buckskin's back. Grunting, he slid the meat off, lifting it onto the bay. The bay snorted and danced sideways at the sudden burden and the close smell of blood. The Indian spoke gruffly to his horse, and it quieted. Then he lifted the bulging leather cases and settled them just in front of the meat, over the bay's withers. Finally he looked up and motioned to Willow, a quick, intricate movement. She shook her head, still not understanding.

The Indian took her hand, ignoring Fancy's startled bark when he came close. He placed the single rein of the buckskin's rawhide hackamore in her hand and closed her fingers around it. His palm was warm and rough, like her father's had been. He gestured toward the river.

This time there was no mistaking what he meant. Willow held the leather rein so tightly that it dug into her hand. She had seen horses swim rivers, though never one as high as this one was, and never carrying a rider. Could she stay on without a saddle? How could she carry Fancy?

The Indian gestured again, saying a few words in his own language, short, impatient words. He took Willow's hand in his again and pulled her along. The horses followed. Fancy, his eyes wide with interest and suspicion, lifted his muzzle and sniffed the unfamiliar scents of the Indian and his horses.

At the water's edge, the Indian dropped the bay's rein and motioned for Willow to wade into the water. He followed, the buckskin coming along docilely, seemingly content to stand in belly-deep water while the Indian talked to Willow, gesturing.

Willow shook her head, terrified and confused. Did he expect her to swim the horse over? Was he going to *make* her? She stared at the water, hating it, shivering at its cold touch as her skirts soaked through.

The Indian made a fork of two fingers on his right hand and set them astride his left. He patted the buckskin's back. Willow let him lift her up, awkwardly swinging her leg over the buckskin, holding Fancy tightly. The buckskin shifted beneath her as her skirts dripped rivulets of water down its sides. The Indian looked at Fancy for a moment, then turned and waded back to the bay. When he came back a moment later, he had a long leather thong.

Willow caught her breath as the Indian fashioned a loop that he slipped around Fancy's neck. Fancy might have bitten him if he had been slow, but the Indian's hand came and went as quickly as a snake. The Indian handed the thong to Willow. Then he stepped behind the buckskin.

Willow watched, mystified, as the Indian lifted the buckskin's long black tail, holding it the way a child playing pony would hold imaginary reins. The buckskin shifted beneath her again, rippling its skin to discourage a deerfly from landing on its withers. The Indian spoke a single, sharp word, and Willow shook her head, baffled by the Indian's pantomime, distracted by the wide river rushing past.

The Indian pulled the little blue bottle from his pouch again. He touched it, then laid his hand on the buckskin's rump. "Trade." His voice was low, final. Willow nodded tentatively.

Then, without warning, the Indian lashed the buckskin's flank with his rein, whooping, startling it farther into the water. He whipped it three or four more times, screeching like a soul from hell. The frightened buckskin lunged forward a second time, slow and ponderous because of the water, then once more to escape the stinging lash. It began to swim. Willow felt the solid ground disappear from beneath its hooves and tangled one hand in its mane, clutching Fancy with the other. The horse sank deeper in the water, swimming with its neck extended, its breath coming harder as the current took hold of them. The buckskin snorted water from its nostrils, struggling, its breath hard and quick.

Willow twisted around to look desperately at the Indian. He was standing beside his horse and turned to grasp the end of its tail, making swimming motions with his free hand. Willow stared, finally understanding.

She tied Fancy's thong to her wrist, then forced herself to swing one leg over the horse's withers, as though she was riding sidesaddle. She counted to ten, then arched her back and slid into the water, holding the horse's mane with one hand and its rein and Fancy with the other. Then she froze. The buckskin was swimming strongly, rising in the water now that Willow's weight was off its back.

Willow hung onto its mane for a few seconds more, afraid to move, afraid the brown water would find a way to swallow her after all. The buckskin rolled its eyes and one of its forehooves grazed her leg. Willow cried out in pain. It was stupid and dangerous to stay where she was.

Willow gathered her courage. What the Indian had told her to do made perfect sense. Heart slamming at her ribs, Willow worked her way along the horse's flank, letting out the rein as she went, pleading with Fancy to stop wriggling.

Taking in a deep, shaky breath, Willow let Fancy go in the water and swam a half stroke and caught at the horse's tail. She let her feet rise, lying forward in the water so that the horse could pull her as easily as possible. She had expected to have to hold Fancy somehow, but he had a better idea. He scrambled up out of the water onto her back.

Willow fixed her eyes on the far bank, praying. The current roared around them, pulling them downstream as the buckskin slowly and steadily moved them across the water. Willow kicked her feet and was careful to keep the rein slack. The sky was lightening as sunrise came closer, and Willow scanned the upstream river nervously as they reached midchannel. But she saw no branches, no drowning trees this time.

When the buckskin had crossed the worst of the current, Fancy spotted the far bank and began to bark. This startled the buckskin, and it swam faster, its breath coming like rhythmic gusts of wind.

When the buckskin's hooves touched bottom, Willow stood, reaching behind herself to catch Fancy as he clambered down her back. He leapt into the water, swimming the last fifty feet on his own, dragging the thong behind him. Willow waded out beside the buckskin, holding the rein tightly. Her knees were trembling, but she smiled, turning to wave at the Indian, a huge triumphant arc of her hand so he would be able to see. He waved back, swung up onto his horse behind the haunch of venison, waved again, then wheeled his bay around and started off. He did not look back.

Willow watched until he disappeared. Fancy ran in circles around her feet, happy and excited to be across. The buckskin shivered the water from its coat, shaking hard to fling the droplets from its mane, switching its tail. Willow bent to untie the thong around Fancy's neck. She wrapped it around her waist, tying it loosely. Then she did her best to wring out her skirts again.

With Fancy trotting along beside her, Willow led the buckskin along the riverbank, heading upstream until she stood again in the wagon tracks and hoofprints of her wagon train, her family. Using a fallen log as a step, she hiked her skirts up around her waist and mounted the buckskin again, then pulled the wet cloth back down to cover her legs. It was odd riding without a saddle, but the buckskin's sides were warm, and Willow was so happy she began to sing quietly as she rode. Fancy came alongside as she turned the buckskin to follow the wagon tracks across the prairie.

Willow had been riding about an hour when she saw a rider approaching. She whistled at Fancy and leaned down. Fancy stood uncertainly, then leapt into her arms. Willow settled him on her lap.

Was it another Indian? This one wouldn't owe her mother a favor of kindness. Willow pulled her buckskin to one side, angling away from the other rider. He responded by urging his horse into a lope. At that moment the sun came fully above the horizon and spread like quick fire across the prairie. Willow stared. The rider was not an Indian. And he was waving at her, urging his horse into a gallop. Willow blinked. It was Mr. Hansen.

The buckskin shied as Mr. Hansen pulled his horse to a stop a few dozen feet away. "Willow," he shouted. "Thank God!" Then he lowered his voice, grinning at her. "Your mother," he said slowly, "is going to be the happiest woman on earth this morning."

He dismounted and came to stand beside her. "Are you all right?"

She managed to nod and smile.

He grinned in response, taking in the buckskin, her muddy clothes, the thong around her waist. "An Indian pony? Well, I think I will wait to hear the story when you tell your mother." He reached up to touch her cheek. "It's just a miracle to see you, Willow." He frowned suddenly. "That's quite a bruise. Are you sure you're all right?" Willow nodded.

Mr. Hansen remounted and turned his horse. He waited for Willow to ride up alongside. She cleared her throat, afraid to ask but compelled to. "Anna? Is Anna . . . ?"

"She is fine," Mr. Hansen said quickly. "And all the rest."

Willow felt a weight leave her heart. "The towrope didn't break?"

Mr. Hansen shook his head. "It didn't. One of the Banner children nearly drowned in the shallows, everyone was so scared and confused getting off, but we got her out in time. We thought we'd lost you, though."

Willow smiled at him again. We, he'd said. *We*. She looked back at the river. The brown water was snaking its way northeast, headed back to where they had come from. Mr. Hansen leaned to pat Fancy's head. "I even missed him." Willow did not trust herself to speak. She was afraid she would start to sob. "Anna and your brothers will be so glad to have you home with us again," Mr. Hansen said, looking at her. Willow nodded, her eyes stinging with tears. That was where she wanted to be. With her family. Home.

June 4, 1847,
Across the South Platte River, Kansas Territory

We made fifteen miles today. I am very tired and will not write long before my eyes begin to close, I am sure. Anna says that since she saw me get pulled into the river, seeing me ride up with our stepfather this morning was like watching someone rise from a grave. Anna was almost swept into the river, too. It was Mrs. Banner who kept hold of her own little ones and also somehow helped my mother hang onto the plank cot until the ferry swung around far enough to let the tree past.

There were no clouds at all tonight, so we are out around the cookfire, which is where I sit to write in this journal. We will sleep in tents or under the wagon, even Anna. Hallelujah! Levin and Jordan are playing checkers. They will start to argue soon; they always do. Then Jordan will be after one of us girls as an easy mark. Well, he won't get me this evening. I would fall asleep while he jumped all my pieces and claimed a victory.

Levin is jealous of my having a horse. I told him it belongs to Mama, if anyone, but Mama and my stepfather say I may keep it. It is a mare, very tame and willing. She is still tired from her swim and followed behind the wagon all day at oxen's pace.

Mother told me how Mr. Hansen insisted on going back for one more look, just to make sure that I hadn't somehow gotten out of the river on my own. The other men tried to discourage him, Mama says, and I could see how proud and grateful she was that he did not heed them. I am grateful, too, and today feel more his stepdaughter than I ever have before.

The piano made it across the South Platte River, and this evening Mrs. Snyder is playing to regale us all with her joy at keeping it for another few miles. She really does play beautifully. If we can just discourage her from singing later, the evening will have been perfect.

Maybe California will be everything that my mother and stepfather hope it will be. It was my father's dream to go there, too. Mr. Campbell talked tonight about the gentle climate and told us how orange trees stay green all year round. I can't wait to see this wonderful place. Perhaps it is becoming my dream, too.